The Camp Fire Girls in the Outside World

Margaret Vandercook

Contents

THE CAMP FIRE GIRLS IN THE OUTSIDE WORLD

BY

Margaret Vandercook

CHAPTER I
"DO YOU REMEMBER ME?"

Walking slowly down a broad stairway, a girl carried three old silver candlesticks in her hands. And although the hallway was in semi-darkness, the candles had not yet been lighted. It was a cold November afternoon and the great house was chill and silent.

Entering the drawing room, she placed the candles upon the mantelpiece. Her breath was like a small gray cloud before her; and her dress, too, was the color of the mist and soft and clinging.

"Work, health and love," she murmured quietly, striking a match and watching the candles flicker and flare until finally they burned with a steady glow. "If one has these three things in life as I have, what else is worth worrying over?" Then the sigh that came in answer to her own question almost extinguished the candle flames.

"There are bills and boarders of course--too many of the first and at present none of the second," she added with a kind of whimsical smile. "But, oh dear, what a trying Thanksgiving day this has been, when even the Camp Fire ideals won't comfort me! Dick 'way off in Germany, Polly and Esther studying in New York and me face to face with my failure to save the old house. It is not worth while pretending; the house must be sold and mother and I shall have to find some other place to live. In the morning I will go and tell Judge Maynard that I give up."

Sadly Betty Ashton glanced about the familiar room. The portraits of her New England ancestors appeared to gaze coldly and reproachfully down upon her. They had not been of the stuff of which failures are made. Her grand piano was closed and dusty, the window blinds were partly pulled down, and although a fire was laid in the grate, it was not burning. Dust, cold and an unaccustomed atmosphere of neglect enveloped everything.

With a lifting of her head and a tightening of her lips that gave her face a new expression, the girl suddenly pulled open a table drawer and began fiercely to polish the top of the piano while she talked.

"There is no reason why I should allow this place to look so dismal just because things have gone wrong with my efforts to keep boarders and continue my work at school. As no one is coming to see me I can't afford a fire, but I'll open the piano and place Esther's song, 'The Soul's Desire,' on the music rack, just as though she were at home to sing it for me. Dick's dull old books shall lie here on the table where he used to leave them, near this red rose that John Everett brought me this morning. Somehow the rose makes me think of Polly. It is so radiant. How curious that certain persons suggest certain colors! Now Polly is often pale as a ghost, and yet red always makes me recall her."

A few moments afterwards and Betty moved toward the front window and stood there staring out into the street, too deep in thought to be actually conscious of what she was doing.

She had changed in the past six months of struggle with poverty and work beyond her strength. There were shadows under her gray eyes and worried lines about the corners of her mouth. Instead of being slim as formerly, she was undeniably so thin that even the folds of her delicate crepe dress could not wholly disguise it.

It was not that Mrs. Ashton and Betty had spent this lonely day in their old home, because their former friends had neglected them. Indeed, they had had invitations to Thanksgiving dinners from half a dozen sources. But Mrs. Ashton had not been well in several months and was today too ill for her daughter to leave her. The two women were now entirely alone in the house. One by one their boarders had deserted them, and the previous week they had even felt compelled to give up the old cook, who had been in the service of the Ashton family for twenty years.

At first Betty saw nothing to attract her attention in the street outside--not a single passer-by. It was odd how quiet and cold the world seemed with her mother asleep in one of the far-away rooms upstairs and other persons evidently too much interested in indoor amusements to care for wandering through the dull town.

In another instant, however, the girl's attention was caught by the appearance of a figure which seemed to spring up suddenly out of nowhere and to stand gazing intently toward the Ashton house. It was almost dark, and yet Betty could distinguish a young man, roughly dressed, wearing no overcoat, with his coat collar turned up and a cap pulled down over his eyes. Without being frightened, she was curious and interested. Why should the man behave so queerly? He now walked past the house and then turned and came back, not once but several times. Evidently he had not observed the girl at the window. At last however he gave up, and Betty believed that she saw him disappear behind the closed cottage of the O'Neills. No longer entertained, she prepared to leave the drawing room. It was too chilly to remain there any longer. Moreover, studying the familiar objects she had loved so long only made the thought of their surrender more painful. Betty once more faced her three candles.

"Be strong as the fagots are sturdy;
Be pure in your deepest desire;
Be true to the truth that is in you;"

"And--follow the law of the fire," she repeated with a catch in her breath. Then with greater strength and resolution in her face she blew out two of the candles, and picking up the third, started on her way upstairs.

The next moment there came a quick, muffled ring at the front door bell.

The girl hesitated; yet there was no one else in the house to answer the bell, and only a friend, she thought, could come at this hour. Shading her light from the wind with one hand she pulled open the door with the other, already smiling with pleasure at the idea of thus ending her loneliness.

Close against the door she discovered the young man whom she had seen only a few moments before in the street.

He did not speak nor move immediately.

"What do you wish?" Betty demanded a trifle impatiently. The fellow had both fists rammed deep into his pockets and had not the courtesy to remove his hat. With a slight sense of uneasiness, Betty thought of closing the door. The unexpected visitor kept edging closer toward her and was apparently fumbling for something in his coat.

"Please tell me what it is you want at once," the girl repeated almost angrily. "This is Mrs. Ashton's house if you are looking for it. My mother and I are entirely alone." Having made this speech Betty instantly recognized its stupidity and regretted it.

However the young man had at last succeeded in removing a small oblong package from his pocket, which he silently thrust toward her. On the wrapper in big letters, such as a child might have written, the girl was able to decipher her own name. But while she was puzzling over it, and before she could thank the messenger, he had hurried off.

Betty set her candle down on the lowest of the front steps and kneeling before it rapidly undid her parcel. Inside the paper she discovered a crudely hand-carved wooden box, and opening the lid, a blank sheet of folded white paper.

She shook the paper. Had some one sent her a Thanksgiving present or was she being made the victim of a joke? But from between the blank sheets something slowly fluttered to her feet. And picking it up with a little cry of surprise Betty saw a crisp new ten dollar bill.

Immediately her cheeks turned scarlet and her eyes filled with indignant tears. Only by an effort of will could the tears be kept from falling. Did any one of her friends consider her so poverty-stricken that it was necessary to send her money in this anonymous fashion?

Scarcely waiting to think, Betty rushed out of the house and down the old paved brick walk out into the street. For there might be a bare chance that the messenger was not yet out of sight. Sure enough, there he was still loitering on the corner about half a block away. Bareheaded, and in her thin dress, with the money in her hand, the girl ran forward. And actually as she reached the young man, she caught him fast by the sleeve.

"Please, you must tell me who sent me this money or else take it back at once and say that though I am very much obliged I cannot receive a gift delivered in this secret fashion."

The two young people were standing near an electric light so that they could now see each other plainly. Betty observed a tall, overgrown boy with thin, straight features and clear hazel eyes, and now that his hat was removed, a mass of curly dark hair, which had been vainly smoothed down.

"I can't take the money back, since it belongs to you," the young man answered awkwardly.

Inside her Betty heard a small voice whispering: "If it only really did!" For the ten dollars would buy Christmas presents for her mother, for Polly and Esther and others of her friends. Nevertheless she shook her head.

"The money cannot be mine and so you must return it." Then finding that her insistence was failing to have any effect, she dropped the money on the ground at the young fellow's feet and walked away.

"But, Miss Ashton," the stranger's voice argued, "please believe me when I say that this money is yours. Oh, of course I don't mean this special ten dollar bill; for yours was spent nearly a year ago. But at least the money represents the same amount."

Betty paused and again faced the speaker. There was sincerity in his tone--a determined appeal. But what on earth could he be talking about? He looked perfectly rational, although his statement was so extraordinary.

"You don't recognize me and I am truly glad," the young man went on. "But can't you recall once having befriended a fellow when instead you ought to have sent him to jail? He did not deserve your kindness then. He was actually trying to steal from you the money which you afterwards gave him of your own free will. But he has tried since to be honest."

He ceased abruptly. For Betty's eyes were shining and she was thrusting her little cold hand into his big one.

"You're not!" she exclaimed.

"Yes I am," the boy returned.

"Anthony Graham, Nan's brother?" Betty laughed happily. "Then please give me back the money I refused. I did not understand that you were returning the loan. Of course I understand how you feel about it. And do come back and into the house with me. I so want you to tell me all about yourself. I hope you have had splendid luck."

The young man's shabby appearance did not suggest sudden riches. Nevertheless he smiled.

For more than ever did Betty Ashton appear to him like the Princess of his dreams. Only once before had he met her face to face. And yet the vision had never left him. He could still see the picture of a girl moving toward him, her face filled with shame--for him--and her eyes downcast; and thrusting into his clenched fist, which had so lately been raised to injure her, the money which had given him the desired opportunity for getting away from his old associations and beginning again.

Enter her home and tell her of his struggle! Anthony felt far more like kneeling in the dust at her feet. Yet being a boy he could only blush and stammer without words to voice his gratitude.

Betty was beginning to shiver. "Please come, I am so lonely," she urged. "I have had the horridest kind of a Thanksgiving day. Only a little while ago I was having a hard time trying to remember the things that I have to be thankful for."

CHAPTER II
BETTY'S KNIGHT

The drawing room fire was soon crackling. "It is so nice to feel I have the privilege of lighting it; I have been dying to for the past hour, but didn't think I could afford it without company," Betty confided, blowing at the flames. "Do please get some chairs and let us draw up quite close. It is so much pleasanter to talk that way."

Yet Anthony Graham only stared without moving. To think of a Princess speaking of not being able to afford so inexpensive a luxury as a fire. Suddenly the young man longed to be able immediately to chop down an entire forest of trees and lay it as a thank offering before her. Of course his sister Nan had written him of Mr. Ashton's death and of the change in the family fortunes, but to associate real poverty with his conception of Betty was impossible. Glancing uneasily about the great room it was good to see how beautiful it still looked, how perfect a setting for its young mistress. So at least they were able to keep their handsome home.

To the young man Betty Ashton now appeared more beautiful than his former impression of her. For on the day of their original meeting she had worn a fur coat and a cap covering her hair and a portion of her face. But now the three Camp Fire candles were once more burning, forming a kind of shining background for the girl's figure. Her hair was a deep red brown, with bronze tones, the colors in the autumn woods. There was no longer any sign of pallor or weariness in her cheeks, for pleasure and excitement had reawakened the old Betty.

"Do sit down," she urged again. "I want to hear all about you."

Then, coming to his senses, Anthony managed to drag two comfortable chairs before the blaze.

"There isn't anything much to tell," he began shyly. "Only after you gave me that money I just started walking farther and farther away from Woodford. Why, it seemed to me that I didn't ever want to stop, for that would give me a chance to realize what I had done. And I didn't stop, either, until I was too dead tired to go on. But by that time I had come to another town and it must have been pretty late, because the main street was empty. I was passing along close to the wall of a building when I saw that an office door had been left open. It was pretty cold, so I peeped in. The room was dark and there was nobody about, so creeping inside I lay down on the floor and went to sleep." The boy stopped, but his listener was leaning forward with her hands clasped and her lips parted with eagerness.

"Do go on and tell me every detail. It sounds just like a story," she entreated.

"When I woke up it was daylight and I found that I had landed in a dusty, untidy place, littered with old books and papers," he continued. "A small stove in the corner was choked up with ashes. I can't tell exactly why, but the first thing I did that morning was to scrape out those ashes, and then I found some sticks and coals and built a fresh fire." Anthony flashed a glance at Betty out of his shy, almost frightened blue eyes. "I guess I was feeling kind of well disposed toward fires just then, camp fires anyhow. Then I was thinking that I would like to pay for my night's lodging in some way. I fell to brushing out the room, so that when the young man came down later he would find his office cleaned up. Seemed like all of a sudden, after what had happened between you and me, that I wanted to work and pay my own way. I had never before been anything but a loafer."

"But you couldn't have known that the office belonged to a young man unless you waited there until after he came in!" Betty exclaimed.

Anthony laughed. "Oh, yes, I waited all right and I have been in that same office more or less ever since, until I came home to Woodford the day before yesterday. Of course I meant to clear out as soon as I had finished, but while I was working I heard a quiet chuckle behind me, and swinging around, there stood Mr. Andrews!"

"But who was or is this Mr. Andrews?" Betty asked impatiently, too interested to be particularly polite.

"My next best friend, after you," the young fellow answered. "Why, I think I can remember even now his very first words to me: 'Hello,' he said, 'why are you doing me such a good turn?' 'Because you have just done me one. I slept all night in your office,' I answered. He didn't seem surprised and I thought that rather funny. But afterwards I learned that he had been a poor boy himself and had slept in all sorts of queer places. He is still poor enough, goodness knows, but he has graduated in law and set up an office. He will succeed some day, sure as faith. You can bet on him."

Betty bit her lips, her eyes dancing with amusement and curiosity. Actually her visitor was becoming so much in earnest over his friend that he was forgetting to be afraid of her.

"But what about you and your success?" she demanded.

The young man flushed, moving uncomfortably in his chair, as though yearning to get away from his questioner, and yet not knowing exactly how.

"Success, *my* success? I haven't yet used that word in connection with myself. I have just managed to keep on working, that's about all. Mr. Andrews let me continue sleeping in his office after I told him my story and cleaning it to pay for my lodging. Then by getting up early enough I arranged to take care of a few others for money and to run errands now and then. I read in between times."

"Read? Read what?" Betty inquired inexorably, half smiling and half frowning at her own persistence. For somehow in their half hour's talk together she had seen something in Anthony Graham that made her guess that the young man had worked harder and dreamed better in this past year than he was willing to acknowledge to her.

But Anthony got up from his chair and began deliberately backing toward the door. He seemed suddenly to have became more awkward and self-conscious. "I read the law books, as there wasn't anything else to read. And I was determined to get more education so that in the future Nan need not be ashamed of me. Afterwards I went to night school and----"

"So you have made up your mind to be a lawyer yourself some day." Betty sighed with satisfaction. How very like a book his confession sounded! She wanted to get more information from her visitor and yet at the same time longed to rush upstairs and commence a letter to Polly O'Neill at once. Wouldn't Polly be interested? For she had predicted on the day of their first meeting that the young man would either turn out to be absolutely no good, or else (and here Betty blushed, recalling the prophecy) "Remain your faithful knight to the end of the chapter."

"But why did you come back to Woodford if this Mr. Andrews was befriending you and giving you a chance?" she inquired, fearing that her illusion might now be shattered.

The young man did not reply at once.

And he scowled until Betty had an uncomfortable recollection of the expression which she had seen on his face the day of his attack upon Polly and her.

Then after moving a few steps nearer the fire so that he and the girl were once more facing each other, Betty could see that his scowl had been due to embarrassment and not anger.

"You are awfully good to be willing to listen to so long a tale of a ne'er-do-well," he returned. "I came back to Woodford because I was determined to make good in my own town. A fellow that can't trust himself in the face of temptations isn't worth being trusted. I'm going back to Mr. Andrews later, perhaps, but this winter I am to stick right here in Woodford and live down my bad name if I can. Judge Maynard says he will give me the same kind of a chance that Mr. Andrews did, if I am worth it. And I shall be able to see Nan and the others now and then. It didn't seem fair for me to be leaving all the family troubles to a girl."

Involuntarily Betty clapped her hands. She had not intended to express her emotion openly, but so pleased was she with Anthony's reply that she couldn't help it. The next moment she felt a little ashamed of her enthusiasm.

"Oh, Nan is equal to almost anything; we consider her the greatest success in our Camp Fire club," Betty protested. "Nan is studying domestic science at the High School and intends teaching it some day, so she will make you awfully comfortable at home."

The young man put out his hand. "Good-bye," he said. "I never dreamed I would be brave enough to ask you to shake hands with me for a good many years yet. But since you have been kind enough----"

"To ask you ten thousand questions," Betty laughed, rising and putting out both hands with a friendly gesture, and then moving toward the door with her caller.

"I am not going to be able to live at home, however," Anthony concluded. "It is too far to our little place to get into town early enough for my work and to be here in the evenings for the night school. I've got to find a room somewhere. I oughtn't to kick because nobody seems crazy to let me stay in their house. I did leave a pretty poor reputation behind me around here and I've got to *show* people first that I mean to behave differently. I guess I'll strike better luck later."

Although Betty was extremely sympathetic, she did not answer at once. For a sudden surprising understanding had come to her. How difficult it must be for any one to have to go about telling his acquaintances of his reformation before having the chance to prove it. Then an almost appealing expression crept into her face, making her cheeks flush hotly and her lashes droop. Her old friends would have recognized the look. For it was the one that she most often wore when she desired to do another person a kindness and feared she might not be allowed.

"Couldn't you, won't you come here and have a room with us?" she asked unexpectedly. "We have such heaps of rooms in this old house and now mother and I are here alone, we really would like to have you for protection. And if you don't like to accept with just my invitation, will you come in again tomorrow or next day? I am sure mother will wish to ask you too."

Anthony Graham had had rather a rough time always. He had a peculiar disposition, and all his life probably liked only a few people very deeply. His wasted youth--nearly twenty years of idling rather than study or work--and his mixed parentage--the Italian peasant mother and his New England father--would make his struggle in the world a long and an uphill one even if he should finally succeed. Among the first things he meant to learn was not to show his emotions too easily, to hide his feelings whenever he could, so that he might learn to take without apparent flinching the hard knocks that life was sure to send. He had been preparing himself for the unkindnesses. Now at Betty's words he felt a lump forming in his throat and had a terrified moment of believing that he was about to cry like a girl. For could it be possible that any human being could so forgive one's sins as almost to forget them? Yet here was Betty Ashton asking him to stay in her home to protect her mother and herself when his only other meeting had been his effort to rob her.

Anthony set his teeth. "I can't live in so grand a house as this. I couldn't afford it," he replied huskily.

It was on the tip of Betty's tongue to protest that she had never dreamed of Anthony's paying anything. For Betty Ashton, whatever the degree of her poverty, could never fail in generosity, since generosity is a matter not of the pocketbook but of the spirit. However, all of a sudden she appreciated that the young man had quite as much right to his self-respect as she had to hers.

"Even the little will be a help to mother and me," she returned more humbly than any one else had ever before heard her speak.

"But perhaps I could be useful. Maybe you haven't so many servants as you once had----"

Anthony stopped, for Betty's expression had changed so completely. Of course she had already repented of her offer.

"We have no servants and you could help a great deal," she answered. And then without any pretense of concealing them, she let two tears slide down her face. "It is only that I had forgotten for the moment that we are not going to be able to stay in our house much longer. We can't afford to keep it for ourselves and I haven't been a success with having boarders. Still it may be some time before we can rent or sell it, and if you will stay here until then----"

Betty winced, for her visitor had this time clasped her hand until the pressure of its hard surface hurt.

"You know it would be the greatest thing that ever happened for me to be allowed to stay here a week," he added.

And Betty laughed. "Then stay."

As she opened the front door another visitor stood waiting on the outside. He was almost as unexpected as Anthony Graham. For it was Herr Crippen, the German music professor and Esther's father.

"What on earth could he want?" Betty thought irritably. She was beginning to feel anxious to get upstairs to her mother again. For in spite of the fact that she now believed that she had a real affection for Esther, she had never been able to recover from her first prejudice for this shabby, hesitating man. Then his manner toward her was always so apologetic. Why on earth should it be? She was always perfectly polite to him. What a queer combination of Thanksgiving visitors she was having!

"Gnaediges Fraeulein," he began. And Betty ushered him into the drawing room. For perhaps he was bringing her news of Esther.

CHAPTER III
HER PENSION

"Good luck never rains but it pours, as well as bad luck, mother," Betty Ashton said one morning nearly a week later. She had just put down a big tray of breakfast on a small table before Mrs. Ashton and now seated herself on the opposite side.

Mrs. Ashton sighed. "If your good luck storm has any reference to us, Betty dear, I am sure I don't get your point of view. For if anything but misfortune has followed our footsteps since your father's death I am sure I should like to hear what it is." And Mrs. Ashton shivered, drawing her light woolen shawl closer about her shoulders.

There are some persons in this world whom troubles brace. After the first shock of a sorrow or calamity has passed they stand reinforced with new strength and new courage. These are the world's successful people. For after a while, ill luck, finding that it can never down a really valiant spirit, grows weary and leaves it alone. Then the good things have their turn--health, better and more admiring friends, fame, money, love. Whatever the struggle has been made for, if it has been sufficiently brave and persistent, the reward is sure. But there are other men and women, or girls and boys, for age makes no difference, who go down like wilted flowers in the teeth of the first storm. And on them life is apt to trample, misfortunes to pile up.

Mrs. Ashton was one of these women. She had made things doubly hard for Betty and Dick. Indeed, except for his sister, Richard Ashton would never have had the strength of purpose to sail for Germany to complete his medical studies. He would simply have surrendered and commenced his practice of medicine in Woodford without being properly equipped for perhaps the greatest of all the professions-

-the struggle to conquer disease. Yet somehow Betty had had a clearer vision than can be expected of most girls of her age. In a vague way she had understood that it is oftentimes wiser to make a present sacrifice for some greater future gain. So she had persuaded Dick to use the little money that he had for his work, assuring him that she and her mother could get on perfectly well together at home. And with half a dozen summer boarders at the time of his leaving, it did look to Dick as though her confidence was not misplaced.

Now in answer to her mother's speech Betty said nothing at first. So that several tears sliding down Mrs. Ashton's cheeks watered her hot buttered toast.

"I am sure I never expected to live to see this day, my dear, when you would have to cook your own breakfast and mine before you could leave for school," she murmured. "Why, I never thought that you would have to turn over your hand even to look after yourself. Until you developed that Camp Fire enthusiasm you had not been taught a single useful thing. After all, perhaps it might have been better for you if I had never been your mother, if----"

Betty laughed teasingly. "My dear Mrs. Ashton, you talk as if you could have avoided that affliction! You could not very well have helped being my mother, could you? You did not deliberately choose me out from a lot of girls. Because if you did, I should have very little respect for your good judgment. Think, if you might have selected either Polly or Esther! Why, then you would be sure to be rich again some day. For one of them would act so marvelously that she would be able to cast laurels at your feet, while the other would sing you back to fortune. But as it is, you will just have to put up with poor me until Dick gets his chance. Now do eat your breakfast while I relate the details of our good luck storm. In the first place, we are not going to have to give up our beloved house. At least not yet, and perhaps never if our German-American Pension plan turns out satisfactorily."

Betty drank a swallow of coffee, hardly appreciating what she was doing, so deep was her absorption in their affairs.

"Honestly, mother, I should never have dreamed of being so interested in this plan of Rose's and Miss McMurtry's for us, if it had not been for Dick's letters. But if German ladies can keep successful pensions, why not Americans? Remember what a funny lot of people Dick has described--the fat widow with the two musical daughters. I hope one of them won't set her cap for Dick, he loves music so dearly.

Then you know the young boy student who was nearly starving when Dick rescued him, and the old Baron who wears a wig, and the half dozen others? But no matter how queer and funny they may be, they can be no more so than our pensioners. There is Miss McMurtry herself and Anthony Graham, and Dr. Barton moving into town to have an office in our old library. I wonder sometimes if he and Rose are still friends. They had a disagreement once out at the cabin and she just speaks to him since."

Then Betty Ashton hesitated and devoted herself to finishing her breakfast.

"I am sure I don't understand why you fail to mention Herr Crippen, child, who is to have a room here with us and teach his pupils in our big drawing room. I am glad he has been so successful with his music pupils that he is able to give Esther the advantage of studying in New York. I wish you did not have such a ridiculous prejudice against him. Indeed, my dear, I have a very strong reason for insisting that you be kind to him. He is Esther's father and----"

Mrs. Ashton spoke more firmly than was usual with her.

But Betty shrugged her shoulders imperceptibly. "Oh, of course I am glad enough to have the Professor here and I have never said I did not like him. But I am specially happy that Edith Norton's family has moved away so she is to have a room with us. I am kind of lonely without Polly and Esther, and somehow Edith,"----Betty broke off abruptly. Not even to her mother did she feel like mentioning the fact that Edith did not seem to be turning out quite so well as the other Sunrise Camp Fire girls.

With a hurried movement she next picked up the breakfast tray, exclaiming:

"Thank heavens we are not going to have to give our lodgers anything but their rooms and that Martha is coming back to do our cooking and the cleaning. Good old soul to offer to do it without pay. She said that she could not bear living anywhere except with us and that she had enough of father's money stored away in bank not to need any more. But we could not have had her work without pay." Betty kissed her mother lightly on the forehead. "If any one else turns up today and wishes a room, just refer them to me. I'm afraid I won't leave us a bed to sleep in. I am getting so anxious to surprise Dick by really earning a lot of money."

"Well, don't rent the back room that Esther used to have, Betty. You may move into it yourself some day if you like, but I would rather not have a stranger occupy it. I----"

"What on earth is queer about that room?" Betty interrupted. "I have not time to listen now, but you **must** tell me. You talk as though it were a kind of Blue-beard's Chamber of Horrors. Yet I don't suppose you would put me in it if I were likely to have my head cut off in consequence. Good-bye, dear." And Betty fled out into the hall, realizing that it must be almost school time.

The door of Esther's old room happened by accident to be standing open, and still holding on to her tray, Betty paused before it for a few moments. She was not thinking of a possible mystery or secret in connection with the room, only wondering if Esther and Polly were to be at home for the Christmas holidays. They both wanted to come, she thought. But Esther was not sure of being able to afford it and Polly was uncertain of whether she wished to stay in her stepfather's house at a time when her stepbrother, Frank Wharton, whom she disliked so much, should also be at home for his holidays. The girl's face was a little wistful. She so longed to see both her friends. Without them and without Dick, this first Christmas under such changed conditions at home might be rather trying.

"Oh!" Betty exclaimed a trifle indignantly, with her arm shaking so that the dishes in her hands rattled dangerously. "What in the world are you doing in the house at this hour, Anthony Graham? You frightened me nearly to death, turning up at my elbow in such an unexpected fashion. I thought you had been gone hours!"

Anthony put down his coal scuttle and took hold of Betty's tray. "I have been away, but I came back for a moment because your mother wished me to do something for her as soon as I had the spare time." His tone was so surly that Betty smiled. Anthony had been brought up with such a different class of people that he was unable to understand sarcasm or pretense of any kind. Whatever one said he accepted in exactly the words in which it was spoken. And Betty and her friends had always been accustomed to joking with one another, to saying one thing, often meaning another. Anthony should have had the sense to realize that she was not really cross, that her indignation was partly assumed. Therefore she did not intend taking the trouble to set him right in the present instance.

"I'll carry the dishes down myself. I have plenty of time," she protested cold-ly.

But Anthony only held the more firmly to the tray, with his face crimsoning.

The truth was that he had been appreciating in the past few days a truth of which the girl herself was as yet unconscious. Betty's manner toward him had noticeably changed. In the excitement of their Thanksgiving day meeting and his romantic return of the money which she had completely forgotten, she had shown far more interest and friendliness than she now did. On that occasion Betty had overlooked the young fellow's roughness, his lack of education and family advantages. Really Anthony had never been taught even the common civilities of life and had to trust to a kind of instinct, even in knowing when to take off his hat, when to shake hands, how to enter or leave a room. And he understood keenly enough his own limitations. Yet the change in Betty's attitude had hurt him, even though he acknowledged to himself his failure to deserve even her original kindness. She was still kind enough of course in the things which she thought counted. She was cordial about his having his room in the house with her mother and herself and most careful of thanking him for any assistance which he rendered them. Yet the difference was there. For neither in heart nor mind had Betty yet grown big enough to feel real comradeship with a boy so beneath her in social position and opportunities.

Nevertheless she did not mean to be ungracious and something in the carriage of the young man's head as he moved off down the hall suggested that he was either hurt or angry, although exactly why Betty could not understand.

"Don't go for a second, Anthony," she called after him. "I wanted to tell you that you are living in a house with a haunted chamber. At least I don't know whether this room is exactly haunted, but there is something queer about it that my mother and brother have never confided to me. Perhaps I shall move in and find out for myself what it is. I will if there is a chance of my friends, Esther Crippen and Polly O'Neill, coming home for the holidays. For it is so big that we could stay in it together. And perhaps Mrs. O'Neill will let Polly come here and visit me for a little while. Both the girls are doing wonderful things in New York City. And I am afraid if they don't come home pretty soon they will both have outgrown me. It is so horrid to be a perfectly ordinary person."

As Betty moved off, the expression on her companion's face did not suggest that he thought of her as entirely ordinary.

CHAPTER IV
TEMPTATION

You are perfectly absurd and I haven't the faintest intention of confiding in any one of you." And Polly O'Neill, with her cheeks flaming, rushed away from a group of girls and into her own bedroom, closing the door and locking it behind her.

This winter at boarding school in New York City had not been in the least what she had anticipated. Perhaps the character of the school she and her mother had chosen had been unfortunate. Yet they had selected it with the greatest care and it was expensive beyond Polly's wildest dreams. For, apart from her own small inheritance, her stepfather, Mr. Wharton, had insisted on being allowed to contribute to her support, and not to appear too ungracious both to her mother and to him, his offer had been accepted. Yet Polly did not consider herself any greater success in thus masquerading as a rich girl than she had been as a poor one. Was she never to be satisfied? Her school companions were all wealthy and few of them had any ideas beyond clothes and society. To them Polly had seemed a kind of curiosity. She was so impetuous, so brilliant, so full of a thousand moods. Betty Ashton had once said that to know Polly O'Neill was a liberal education, and yet in order to know her one ought to have had a liberal education beforehand.

Today during the recreation hour at "Miss Elkins' Finishing School," which was Polly's present abode, there had been a sudden discussion of plans for the future. And Polly, partly because she was in a contradictory mood and partly because she really wished it to be known, had boldly announced herself as poor as a church mouse with no chance of not starving to death in the future unless she could learn to make her own living.

And this had started the onslaught of questions from which she had just torn herself away.

For Polly had absolutely determined not to confide in any one of her new companions her ambition to go upon the stage. They would not understand and would only be stupid and inquisitive. Why, had they not worried her nearly to death simply because of her acquaintance with Miss Margaret Adams? For one day the great actress had driven up to the school and taken Polly for a drive. And ever afterwards the other girls were determined to find out how and when she had met her and what she was like in every smallest particular, until Polly was nearly frantic.

Now in her own room, which was a small one, but belonged to her alone, the girl dashed cold water on her face until she began to feel her temper cooling down. Then with a book in her lap she planted herself in a low chair. The book was a collection of Camp Fire songs which Sylvia Wharton had given her. And although Polly could not sing, the poetry and inspiration of them was so lovely that she felt they might be a consoling influence.

Nevertheless Polly did not commence reading at once. Instead, her thin shoulders drooped forward pathetically, and putting one elbow on her knee she rested her pointed chin in her hand.

For she was unhappy without any real reason in the world. Polly O'Neill was one of the sensitive and emotional persons who must always be more or less miserable in the wrong environment. She did not like being at boarding school and yet she did not wish to return to Woodford to live in her stepfather's house in circumstances so different from those of her old life. Besides, had not Miss Adams advised that she spend several years away from Woodford in order to see more of the outside world and its myriad types of men and women? She could not ask to be allowed to come back home now, after the fight she had made to leave. Moreover, she was learning many things that might be useful to her as an actress. Miss Adams herself had said so. There was no fault with the opportunities for study at Miss Elkins', only with the interest of the girls. She herself was working hard at French and German and physical culture and was having some special private teaching in elocution by a master recommended by Miss Adams.

No, Polly did not intend to give up. Only she was trying to decide whether or not to return to Woodford for the Christmas holidays. She was longing to see her mother and Mollie and Betty Ashton. Yet Frank Wharton would be at home and she and Frank had quarreled all the time that they had been in the house together during the past summer. And her mother and Mollie were so wrapped up in one another and in the splendid new home and in Mr. Wharton! Polly felt herself almost an outsider when she thought of the days when they had lived in their own little cottage just opposite the Princess.

Then, at the thought of Betty Ashton, the slightly hard look in Polly's Irish blue eyes faded. Of the Princess' understanding and affection she could always feel sure. And what a brave fight she was making! Every letter from her mother or Mollie or from any one of their old Camp Fire circle had something admiring to say of her. And yet she and Mollie had always thought of their Princess as only a spoiled darling, beautiful and meant only for cherishing. Ah well, the Princess was really an aristocrat in the old meaning of the word. She had never been in the least like these New York girls, caring for money for its own sake and feeling superior to other people just because of her money. Betty had birth and beauty and brains.

Suddenly Polly dashed the tears from her eyes and with a smile jumped to her feet, dropping her Camp Fire book. There was no use sitting there and thinking of all the virtues that her Princess possessed that began with "b." This was Friday afternoon and she was free to do what she liked. Esther was living in a boarding house not far away, and she had not seen her in two weeks. And in all the world there was nothing Esther liked to talk about so much as Betty. Besides, if Esther were going home for the holidays, why, Polly felt that she would rather like to have some one persuade her into making her own decision.

Is it good or evil fortune that makes one so readily influenced by outside conditions? The December afternoon was cold and brilliant; and in few places is the climate of early winter so stimulating as in New York City. Esther was not at home, and for a few minutes her visitor felt disappointed. But the streets were so beautiful and alluring and there were so many people out! It was true that Polly had received permission only to call upon her friend, but what wrong could there be in her taking a walk? She had only to keep straight along Broadway and there could be no possible chance of getting lost. Polly was not in the least timid or unable to take care of herself. She was a girl from a small town, and yet no one could have imagined that she had not been a New Yorker all her life, except for her quick and eager interest in the sights about her.

No one noticed or molested Polly in the least. It was only that in her usual unthinking fashion she flung herself into the way of temptation. Farther down Broadway than she had ever been before, Polly stopped for a moment to look more closely at a group of girls. Most of them were several years older than herself. They were standing close together near a closed door, and yet only occasionally did one of them make a remark to the other; for apparently they were strangers to one another.

At first the girls themselves attracted Polly's attention because the larger number appeared so nervous and anxious. More than half of them had their faces rouged and powdered and were fashionably dressed, yet even when they smiled their expressions were uneasy.

They interested the country girl immensely. In order not to seem rude or inquisitive she pretended to wish to gaze into a shop window near them. Then, as they continued waiting and showed no sign of what they were waiting for, Polly O'Neill's curiosity overcame her good manners. Another girl had separated herself from the group and was standing within two feet of Polly, also pretending to stare into the same window.

Polly edged closer to her. The young woman must have been nearly twenty-five. She had been pretty once, yet already her face was haggard and she had circles under her big brown eyes. Unexpectedly Polly smiled at her, and there was always something almost irresistible in Polly's smile.

"Could you, would you mind telling me why so many girls are standing here in this one particular spot?" she inquired. "It is a cold day when one is still. And yet I have been here almost ten minutes and no one has even started to move away."

"We are waiting to try to get jobs," the older girl answered listlessly. "And we have come sooner than we were told because each one of us hoped to get ahead of the other."

"Jobs?" Polly repeated stupidly. "What kind of work is it that you are looking for?"

"Oh, theatrical jobs," the young woman explained. "It's coming on to be Christmas time and the managers are putting on extras for the holidays."

She turned away from her questioner, believing that she had heard a faint noise at the door near which they were lingering. A quick tug at her coat attracted her attention again.

"Can any one apply for a position who wants it?" Polly queried. Her eyes were shining, her cheeks were crimson and her breath coming in kind of broken gasps as though she were frightened.

But the magic door had opened at last and the older woman had no time to waste. "Oh, yes, any one can apply," she returned with a kind of hardness. And then she failed to observe that the girl she had been talking with was following close behind her.

Polly herself hardly realized what she was doing. Once more she had yielded to that old wretched habit of hers, of acting first and then thinking afterwards. Like a flash of lightning it had but this instant occurred to her that more than anything she would like to see inside a theatrical manager's office. It would be like placing the tips of one's toes on the promised land. Of course, Polly knew perfectly well that she was being reckless, only she would not allow herself time to consider this point of view. She would simply slip in with these other girls and pretend that she would like a position should she be forced into it. As she had had no experience, there could be no possibility of her getting an engagement. Ten minutes afterwards she would slip out again and return to school.

With a dozen or more other girls, Polly was the next moment ushered into a room that was quite dark and had only a few chairs in it. There they were told to wait until the manager could be free to speak to them. So Polly crowded herself into the farthest, darkest corner and immediately her heart began to thump and her knees to shake, while she wished herself a thousand miles away.

What would her mother say to this latest of her escapades; and Mollie and Betty? What would Miss Adams, for that matter, think of her? She was an actress herself; but of course Polly never imagined that she had started her career in any such humble fashion.

Coming partially to her senses, Polly started hurriedly toward the closed door. There was no reason in the world for her remaining in this room unless she wished it. But just as she turned the knob the manager entered from the hall. And Polly's curiosity got the better of her again. She would stay just half a minute longer and see what happened.

CHAPTER V
THE WAY OF THE WILFUL

When Polly O'Neill came out into the street again, she did not know whether she was walking on the sidewalk, in the air, or at the bottom of the sea. But because of a certain thrilling excitement she felt that she must have wings and because of a heavy weight inside her that she must be in the depth of the sea.

For Polly had just signed an engagement to act for two weeks in a Christmas pantomime.

It sounds incredible. And it was possibly as unwise and headstrong a thing as a girl could well do. And yet Polly had originally no actual intention or desire to do wrong. Simply she had yielded to a sudden impulse, to an intense curiosity. But now things were different; for Polly was realizing her wilfulness completely, and instead of repenting and turning back to confess her folly, was every moment trying to plan by what method her purpose could be accomplished.

Not for anything in the world would her mother give her consent to her experiment. And that in itself should have been a sufficient argument against it. Yet Polly explained to herself that, after all, there could not be any great harm in doing what she so much wished, provided that she made confession afterwards. She was almost eighteen, and thousands of girls in New York City were earning their living, who were years younger than she. Perhaps it might even do her good to find out what this stage life really was like--whether it was as fascinating as she dreamed, or all tinsel as most grown people were so fond of telling her.

No, the question that was uppermost with Polly O'Neill was not in connection with her decision. It was how her decision might best be carried out.

Fortunately she had been writing that she did not believe that she would come home for the Christmas holidays. She did wish to see her mother and Mollie and Betty, of course, and had almost given way to this longing only an hour before. But now, had not fate itself intervened, flinging her into the path of her desire? And Polly was Irish and had always declared that she believed in the leadings of fate, even when her mother and sister had insisted that fate and her own wish were too often confused in her mind.

Had she not hidden herself in the corner when the theatrical manager entered the room, with every intention of running away as soon as she could escape unobserved? And then had he not suddenly swooped down upon her, selecting her from the dozens of other applicants? Polly was not exactly sure of what had happened, except that the man had said that she looked the part of the character he was after. The fact that she had confessed having had no stage experience had not even deterred him. The new play was to be chiefly for young people and the manager particularly required youthful actors and actresses.

The play to be produced was the dramatization of a wonderful old Bohemian fairy story, which Polly remembered to have read years before, called "The Castle of Life." The story is that of a little boy, Grazioso, brought up by his grandmother, whom he loves better than all else in the world. Then one day he sees that the grandmother is growing old and fears that she must soon leave him. And so he sets out to find "The Castle of Life" in order once more to bring back youth to the old woman. The play follows his adventures on the road to the castle, and includes his meeting with two fairies--the Fairy of the Woods and the Fairy of the Water. Polly was to impersonate the wood spirit.

Her appearance did suggest the character, though naturally she could not appreciate this fact. But there was always something a bit eerie and fantastic about her, something not exactly of the everyday world--her high cheekbones and thin, emotional face with its scarlet lips and intense expression faintly foreshadowing an unusual future.

But Polly at the present moment was not feeling in the least unusual, only rather more self-willed and more calculating. Never could she recall having deliberately deceived any one before in her entire life. And yet to accomplish her present purpose there was no other way than the way of deception. No one in Woodford must guess at her reason for remaining in New York during the holidays, nor must

Miss Elkins have any possible cause for suspicion. Of course she could not stay on at boarding school. That idea was utterly ridiculous. She would never be allowed to go out for a single evening alone. Already her right to liberty had been considerably overreached by this walk of hers down town. And what she had done during the walk! The offender smiled rather wickedly at the thought of the consternation and excitement that the discovery of her act would create. Home she would go to Woodford then to stay indefinitely!

But Polly did not mean to be found out, She meant to have her little taste of emancipation and then go back into routine again, until she was old enough for a larger freedom. So for this reason, although she should have returned to school an hour before, she continued walking slowly, devising and rejecting a dozen plans. It was going to be tremendously difficult to accomplish her purpose. But this she had foreseen five minutes after she had promised to accept the theatrical manager's offer. However she would "find a way." She remembered how often the Princess had said that she had more talent than "Sentimental Tommy" in this particular direction.

She reached Miss Elkins' school and received five minutes' scolding from that lady, in the meekest spirit, still without having any idea of what she could possibly do to accomplish her design.

All evening she talked so little and her attention was so concentrated upon the lesson which she appeared to be studying, that her school companions left her entirely alone. Polly's passion for studying had always been regarded as an eccentricity. But now since she had announced on that afternoon that she had her own living to make there was possibly some excuse for her industry. Nevertheless the girls felt more convinced than ever that she was not in the least like any of the rest of them and, although rather fascinating and unusual, not a person whom one would care to know intimately.

The difference in her manner and expression that night attracted the attention of one of the teachers--the girl's face was so tense and white, her blue eyes showed such dark shadows beneath them. It was owing to this teacher's advice that Polly was allowed to leave the study hall an hour earlier than usual and go to her own room and to bed.

She was not feeling particularly well. Her head did ache and her conscience troubled her the least little bit, notwithstanding she had not the faintest intention of surrender. With hot cheeks and cold hands she lay still for a long time until the noises of the other girls retiring had quieted down and the big house was silent. Then Polly suddenly sat up in bed. A moment later she had crawled out on the floor and lighted a candle by her writing desk. The electric lights had been turned off for the night. But even in the pitch darkness Polly would still have composed her letter. For an idea had at last come to her. And if only she could get just one person to accede to it her way would be plain. The one person might be difficult. Polly was perfectly aware of this, but then she had great faith in her own powers of persuasion.

CHAPTER VI
ESTHER'S ROOM

Just above the small alcohol lamp the teakettle was beginning to sing. On a table near-by were teacups and saucers, with one plate of sandwiches covered over with a small napkin, and another of cookies.

Several times a tall girl glanced at the clock and then walked across the room to take the kettle off the stove, only to place it back again the next instant.

Then at last she seated herself by an open piano. There was very little furniture in the room except the piano, a small cot and the table. Yet it had an atmosphere of home and comfort, such as some persons are able to give to a tent in a desert. And standing in a row at the back of the same tea table were three candles in ten-cent-store glass candlesticks, waiting to be lighted. The afternoon was a dismal one, with occasional flurries of snow; so that when the proper time came for the candle-lighting, the flames would not be ungrateful.

But in order to make the waiting seem less long the girl was evidently trying to distract her attention by practicing her music. Several times she sang over the scales. And then, dissatisfied with her own work, repeated them until finally her voice rose with unusual resonance and power. Then, after another slight pause, she drifted almost unconsciously into the words of a song:

"Burn, fire, burn!
Flicker, flicker, flame!
Whose hand above this blaze is lifted
Shall be with magic touch engifted,
To warm the hearts of lonely mortals
Who stand without their open portals.

The torch shall draw them to the fire
Higher, higher
By desire.
Whoso shall stand by this hearthstone,
Flame-fanned,
Shall never, never stand alone;
Whose house is dark and bare and cold,
Whose house is cold,
This is his own.
Flicker, flicker, flicker, flame;
Burn, fire burn!"

She had not heard the door open softly nor even noticed the figure that crept softly into the small room.

But now a pair of gloved hands were clasped eagerly together and an enthusiastic voice said:

"Esther Crippen, that is the loveliest song in all the world and you are the loveliest singer of it! How glad I am to have arrived at just this moment! Why, your little room makes me feel that it is a *real* refuge from all that is dark and bare and cold. And you surely are with the 'magic touch engifted to warm the hearts of lonely mortals' with that beautiful voice of yours."

And Polly O'Neill, putting one hand on each of Esther's cheeks, kissed her with unexpected ardor.

It made Esther flush and tremble slightly as she rose to greet her long-desired guest. Any compliment made Esther shy and one from Polly more than from another person. For although each girl admired the other's talents and character, they had never understood each other especially well. Esther always seemed to Polly far too sober and almost too unselfish and self-effacing, while Polly to the quieter girl had all the brilliance and unreliability of a will-o'-the-wisp. Before coming to New York for the winter their intimacy had been due largely to their mutual devotion to Betty; but now, both lonely and both in a new environment, they had been greatly drawn together. Polly's occasional visits had been one of Esther's few sources of pleasure outside her work.

"How charming you are looking, Polly," Esther began, taking off her guest's dark coat and hat, and seeing her emerge in a crimson woolen dress, which made a bright spot of color in the shabby room. Polly, you must remember, was only pretty on occasions; but this afternoon was certainly one of her good-looking days. The cold had made her pale cheeks flame and given a softer glow to her eyes.

"I am simply ravenous, Esther, and dying for your delicious tea," Polly next remarked, following her hostess to the tea table and taking her seat, while Esther poured out the boiling water. "It is a kind of a homesick day and I have been wishing that we were going to have a meeting of our old Sunrise Hill Camp Fire circle. What wouldn't you give for a glimpse of the Princess this afternoon?"

Esther's lips twitched as she lighted her three candles.

"Almost anything I possess," she returned.

"But you are going to see her pretty soon? You are going back to Woodford for Christmas?" Polly tried to hide her own nervousness in putting this simple question. With her eyes shining over the edge of her cup she continued slowly drinking her tea, so that the rest of her face could not be seen.

But Esther was not paying her any special attention. Quietly she shook her head. "No, Polly, I am not going home. I am so sorry, for I wanted to dreadfully. But my music lessons are so expensive that father does not feel he can afford to let me come. I haven't yet had the courage to write and break the news to the Princess. She is fond of me, don't you think so, Polly? She will be sorry that I can't be with her for the holidays? Of course I know she does not care for me as she does for you. I shall never expect that. But it does mean so much to me to feel sure of her affection."

Polly frowned in a slightly puzzled fashion. Esther's adoration even of her beloved Betty seemed a little unnatural. Why should one girl care so much about the attitude of another one? She loved Betty herself, of course, and Betty loved her. Yet she doubted very much if either one worried over the emotions of the other.

"Oh, yes, Esther," Polly returned a trifle impatiently. "Of course Betty is devoted to you. Why shouldn't she be? Really, I do think you would let her almost trample upon you if she liked. Only Betty never would like to hurt any one, thank heaven! But I am glad to hear you are not going home for the Christmas holidays, because I am not going either."

There was nothing so remarkable in this statement that it should make Polly turn white and then red again. But fortunately the three Camp Fire candles, "Work, Health and Love," were now flickering so that the elder girl could not get a clear vision of the other's face.

But instead of appearing pleased over this news Esther seemed disappointed. "I am so sorry, for Betty's sake," she returned. "She wouldn't mind my not being with her so much if she only might have you."

Polly shrugged her thin shoulders in a fashion she had when vexed.

"O Esther, I think you might have been polite enough to say that you would be glad to have me in town if you were to be here--particularly when I came to ask you if I might spend the holidays with you."

"Spend the holidays with me?" Esther repeated in rather a stupid fashion. Naturally she was puzzled as to just why a girl in Polly's position should elect to spend her Christmas vacation in a cheap New York boarding house with another girl for whom she had no special sentiment.

"Why in the world do you want to remain in the city with me?" she asked again, too honest to pretend that pleasure was her first sentiment until she got a more definite understanding of the situation.

But Polly was now making no effort to devote her attention either to eating or drinking. Instead she had rested both elbows on the table and was looking at her companion with the half-pleading, half-commanding expression that both Mollie and Betty knew so well.

"Promise not to say anything until I have finished?" she began coaxingly. "For you see it is to explain why I want to stay with you that made me write to ask you to make this engagement with me for this afternoon."

CHAPTER VII
THE THREAT

T hen you refuse to help me or to keep my secret?" Polly O'Neill protested indignantly. "Really, Esther, I never knew any one with such a gift for considering herself her sister's keeper. We belong to the same Camp Fire Club. And if that means anything I thought it was loyalty and service toward one another.

"'As fagots are brought from the forest
Firmly held by the sinews which bind them,
So cleave to these others, your sisters,
Wherever, whenever you find them.'"

Esther had walked across the room and had her back turned during this recitation. But now she moved around, facing her visitor until it was Polly's eyes that dropped before her own. The older girl had always the dignity that comes from truth and sincerity.

"Don't be absurd, Polly," she said, speaking quietly, but with no lack of decision. "You know as well as I do that loyalty has nothing to do with aiding one another to do what one does not believe to be right. I don't want to preach. Yet don't you think perhaps *you* are breaking a part of our Camp Fire law? 'Be Trustworthy. This law teaches us not to undertake enterprises rashly.'"

"Oh, please hush, Esther," Polly insisted. "There is no use in our quarreling, and we are sure to if you go on preaching like that. I told you what I have made up my mind to do. If you don't wish to help me, that of course is your affair. All I have the right to demand is, that what I told you in the strictest confidence you repeat to no one else."

She picked up her coat and began slowly buttoning it, waiting for Esther's reply, which did not come at once.

"I don't know whether I can promise you even that," the older girl answered finally. Her face was white and she moved her hands in the old nervous fashion that Betty had almost broken her of. "I don't suppose you can understand, Polly, what an almost dangerous thing you are about to undertake. And without your mother knowing it! O Polly, please don't! Why, if anything should happen to you what would she say to me or Molly and Betty, if knowing your intention I did not warn them?"

Polly was like a hot flame in her anger. In her life Esther scarcely remembered ever having seen any one in such intense yet quiet passion. All the blue seemed to have gone out of her visitor's eyes until they were almost black. Her lips were drawn and although she tried to control her voice, it quivered like a too-tightly-drawn violin string.

"Esther," she said, "I shall not leave this room until I have your solemn promise. Perhaps you don't know anything about the standards of conduct between people of birth and breeding. You were brought up in an orphan asylum and had no mother. Whether you disapprove of me or not makes no difference. I am not objecting to your disapproval. I can perfectly understand that. But what I absolutely will not endure is for you to tell my secret because it happens to strike your conscience that that is the right thing to do. My secret belongs to me as absolutely as my clothes or any of my other possessions do. And because you chance not to approve of it or of them is no reason why you should steal them from me and give them away to other people."

Again Esther was silent and her eyes filled with tears. What was the use of arguing with Polly when she was in this mood? Yet there were so many things that she could honestly say. And one of them, that if she had had the good fortune to have a mother, she at least would not have tried to deceive her as Polly was doing.

However Esther was not sure that the latter part of her companion's argument was not true. Had she the right to betray Polly's confidence, even though she might consider it for her good? For Polly had begun her revelation by insisting that what she told be kept in the strictest secrecy, and she had listened with that understanding.

Unfortunately Esther's failure to reply did not strike her visitor as indicating a change in her point of view. Polly flung herself angrily down into a chair, as though intent upon beginning a siege. She was trying in a measure to control her temper, realizing how ashamed she usually felt after the flare of it was past. Still she did honorably consider that Esther's attitude in the present situation was the wrong one. Perhaps she was being disobedient, wilful, wicked even. Yet she had made up her mind to take the consequences (at least the consequences that she was now able to foresee). And she had no idea of being frustrated in her purpose by an outside person, whose assistance she had been foolish enough to ask. No, some way must be devised that would force Esther into silence.

Polly glanced desperately about the small room. There was a big photograph of the Princess, smiling at her from the wall, the Princess at her loveliest, with her exquisitely refined features, her delicate, high-bred air. She turned away from it rather quickly to look again at her companion. Goodness, what a contrast there still was between the two girls! They had believed that Esther was improving a little in her appearance. Yet just now worry and uncertainty made her seem plainer even than usual. And she had on an ugly but thoroughly useful chocolate-colored dress that Betty would have made her throw into the fire at once.

"Betty, it was always Betty with Esther Crippen!" If only she could reach Esther in some way through their friend. This was an ugly thought of Polly's. She was ashamed of it and yet felt herself driven to using almost any means toward attaining her end.

"Look here, Esther Crippen," she began, breaking the silence first. "I wonder if it has ever occurred to you that you may some day have a secret in your life (or you may have one already for all that I know), which you want more than anything to keep hidden from people. Say you particularly wished Betty never to find it out. Well, suppose I discovered your secret, suppose I knew about it right now, would you want me to tell Betty everything that I had found out just because I decided that it would be the right thing to do?"

Polly happened to be staring into her own lap as she delivered this speech, feeling none too proud of it and having to trust to her imagination as she went along. Now, however, she glanced up into the face of the other girl, who was standing near her.

Then with an exclamation of regret, almost of fear, Polly jumped to her feet.

"Good heavens! Esther, what is the matter with you? Are you ill, do you feel like you were going to faint? If you are sick why on earth haven't you told me before? We could talk over this business of mine any time."

And Polly, forgetting her anger, put her arm reassuringly about her former friend, fairly leading her to a chair. Esther continued staring at her, with a deathly white face, evidently trying to speak, but not able. Then suddenly the girl collapsed and dropping her head on her arm began to cry. She was ordinarily self-restrained; and being brought up in an orphan asylum among people who took no interest in her emotions she had learned unusual self-control. Probably only three or four persons had ever seen her give way like this before in her life. So she did not cry easily, but in a kind of shaken, broken fashion that brought a remorseful Polly on the floor at her feet.

"What on earth have I said that has hurt you so, Esther?" she begged. "I know I am a wretched little beast who does or say 'most anything sometimes in order to get my own way. But of course I don't know any secret of yours and if I did I should never tell. I only like to threaten things because I'm cross. You see I don't believe in telling secrets."

This was a Polly-like way of apologizing and yet driving in her own claim at the same time. If only at this moment Esther had had the Princess' understanding of Polly O'Neill's character, most certainly she would have laughed. But Esther could not pull herself together so quickly. A few moments later, however, she put her hands on Polly's shoulders and in the face of all that had just happened, kissed her.

"No, Polly," she said, "I know that if ever you should make up your mind that there was something, which I thought best should never be known, you would never tell it, even if I betray your secret now. Perhaps we don't agree about some things. But you could never be revengeful. I am sure I don't know what I ought to do. Of course you have the right to choose for yourself. I--I wish you wouldn't do what you have decided upon. But if I don't tell and yet don't let you stay here with me, what on earth would you do about this theatrical scheme?"

"Why, go to some other boarding house for two weeks," Polly replied calmly. "I am sure that is exactly what you are doing, boarding in New York and going on with your work. Of course your work happens to be studying music at present, but you have already sung at two church concerts and----"

This time Esther did laugh. "Well, church concerts are hardly to be compared with the stage, Polly. And please look in your mirror and remember that I am I and you are you. But of course you realize that if you will go on with this whim of yours, I am not going to let you live in any place by yourself. You would be sure to get ill or something dreadful might happen. No, I shall beg you every minute till the time comes, not to do what you must know would worry your mother. But if you still persist, why, you are coming right here to stay with me and I shall be your shadow every moment until you go back to school."

Polly jumped up hastily. "What an impolite suggestion for a hostess!" she murmured, pretending that the seriousness of the situation was now entirely past. "Go back to school? Dear me, that is what I must do this very minute! Good-bye." And kissing Esther hastily on the hair, Polly seized her hat and fled out the door.

Yet halfway down the long stairs the girl hesitated and stopped for an instant as if intending to return.

"Perhaps I ought to give up and be good for once," she whispered to herself. "It won't be fair, and mother and Mollie and Betty may be angry with Esther for not telling. Even if I have the right to get into trouble myself, I haven't the right to drag in other people. But, oh dear! what fun it will be! And with Esther for my duenna, things are sure to turn out all right."

On the lowest steps Polly passed a small boy hobbling up toward Esther's room. He was evidently a boy from the streets, as he was shabbily dressed and carried half a dozen papers under his arm. But there was a hungry, eager look in his face that Polly remembered having seen sometimes in Esther's in those early days of her first coming to Mrs. Ashton's home. So straightway she guessed that the boy was some child, whom Esther had discovered, with a talent and love for music and that she was giving him lessons in her leisure moments.

CHAPTER VIII
PREPARATIONS FOR THE HOLIDAYS

B ut if you won't come, Betty dear, I shan't wish to give the party," Meg
Everett announced in a disappointed fashion. "With Polly and Esther not
to be here, there are so few of our old Camp Fire circle anyhow. And you
see I only wanted to have our club and a few of John's young men friends.
The idea is that we girls are to cook the entire dinner and then just talk or dance or
play games afterwards. It is not to be anything like a *real* party."

Betty smiled. She and Meg and Mollie O'Neill were taking a winter tramp
through the woods in the direction of the Sunrise Cabin, which had been closed for
the past six months.

"I should dearly love to come, Meg," Betty confessed. "There is no use in my
pretending that I shouldn't feel desperately lonely with the thought of your having
such a good time without me. But mother----"

Mollie gave her arm an affectionate squeeze. "There, Betty Ashton, that is just
exactly what I knew you would say. So I talked the whole matter over with your
mother myself first. And she declares that there isn't any reason why you should
not accept Meg's invitation. She is quite sure that your father would never have
wished you not to be as happy as possible. You have had trouble enough, goodness
knows!

And then the extra disappointment of Polly's and Esther's remaining in New
York! I am glad enough Meg is going to give a party, and I hope there will be dozens of delightful things that Polly O'Neill will miss. What on earth do you suppose
has possessed her to want to stay on with Esther?"

And Mollie sighed. The three months without her sister may have passed by
in greater peacefulness than with her, but then Polly always added a zest and flavor

to existence. And this was the longest time that the two girls had ever been separated.

"Oh, I don't know. She must have had some very good reason," Betty returned. "Polly wrote me that she had, and now we must not believe that she did not love us as much as ever. She wasn't able to explain the particulars just at present; but if we only trust her and forgive her some day we will understand."

Mollie frowned. With a much quieter and more amiable temperament than her twin, yet nearly eighteen years of intimate living with her had given her a pretty clear comprehension of her sister's character. Privately Mollie was puzzled over Polly's behavior and a good deal worried. It was not like Polly to have conceived so sudden a devotion to Esther as to be unwilling to leave her for two weeks. And her claim that she might not be particularly happy at home because of her stepbrother's presence was not convincing. For Betty Ashton had invited Polly to be her guest. No, Polly certainly had some special design in staying on in New York. Of this Mollie was completely convinced. But what the purpose was, neither from her own imaginings nor from any hint dropped by her sister's letters, could she get the slightest clue.

The three girls had come to a narrow path through the woods, and for a little while were compelled to walk in single file. For a few moments they were silent, each one busy with her own thoughts, Mollie happening to be in the middle.

"I believe I'll ask Billy what he thinks," she remarked suddenly aloud. And then she bit her lips, blushing until the very tips of her ears grew warm. For Meg and Betty were both laughing in the most ridiculous way.

"Is it as bad as that, Mollie?" Meg teased.

"Ask Billy what he thinks on one or all subjects, dear?" Betty queried.

To both of which questions Mollie naturally deigned no reply.

She and Billy Webster were extremely good friends. Indeed, they seemed always to have been since the day of their first meeting, when she had bound up his injured head. And this winter, with Polly away and Betty so busy and Meg wrapped up in keeping house and Sylvia spending all her spare hours in studying with Dr. Barton when not at school, she had enjoyed the walks and talks with the young man perhaps more than usual. But it was not because of their intimacy that she had considered putting this problem of Polly's failure to return home before him. Her reason was that in their long conversations about her sister, Billy had always seemed not only to be interested in Polly but able to understand her disposition peculiarly well. So it was stupid for her two friends to have taken her foolish exclamation as meaning anything personal.

The next ten minutes Betty and Meg had rather a difficult time in making peace; for Mollie had not a strong sense of humor--a fact which both girls should have remembered. But because she was always so gentle and kind herself, no one of her friends could bear the idea of hurting her feelings under any circumstances.

However while Betty was in the midst of apologizing, Billy Webster himself came swinging along the same path from the opposite direction. He had his gun over his shoulder and half a dozen birds in his hand.

"Who is it taking my name in vain?" he demanded of Betty.

And Mollie had a dreadful moment of fearing that Betty might betray what they had been talking about. However, as nothing of the kind happened, ten minutes later Meg and Betty were walking ahead deep in conversation about the party, while Mollie and Billy strolled after them only a few feet behind.

The young man had been on his way into Woodford to divide the product of his day's hunting between Mrs. Ashton and Mrs. O'Neill. Now, hearing that the girls were on a pilgrimage to Sunrise Cabin, he had been invited to accompany them.

"No, it won't be like a meeting of our Camp Fire Club, Meg," Betty argued thoughtfully, after having satisfied herself by a glance over her shoulder that Mollie and Billy were too absorbed in each other to take any notice of them. "I have been coming to our Camp Fire Club meetings all winter and because I am in mourning made no difference. But with John inviting his friends to your entertainment, why, I can't make up my mind yet, dear, whether I have the courage to come."

Betty spoke bravely, but Meg slipped her arm across her friend's shoulder, holding her fast. The two girls were closer friends now that Polly and Esther were both away and Meg understood that sometimes Betty did not feel so cheerful as she pretended.

"John won't ask more than just one other fellow to keep him company, if we can have you with us in no other way," Meg conceded. "You see, Betty, John is only to be at home for a few days. As this is his senior year at college he wants to so some special work during the holidays. But he likes you so much better than any of the other girls in Woodford, that I am quite sure----"

But Betty had stuffed her fingers in her ears and was refusing to listen. "It is bad enough to have you girls spoil me because I am in trouble, but when it comes to telling fibs I won't hear you. Of course you know, Meg Everett, that I am not going to let you spoil everybody's pleasure on my account," she answered.

Feeling the victory already won, Meg laughed. "John is only to invite Billy Webster and Frank Wharton and Ralph Bowles and three or four of his Boy Scout camp. By the way, Betty, one of the things I particularly wished to talk to you about is this: Shall we ask Anthony Graham? He seems rather uncouth and the other fellows won't have anything to do with him. But he is Nan's brother and she is so splendid I should hate to hurt her feelings."

Betty shook her head. "Anthony isn't the kind of person to invite though, Meg," she replied without a moment's hesitation. "Of course he is trying to pull up and keep straight and I feel that we should do all we can to help him. But inviting him to our parties and treating him as if he were exactly our equal!" Betty's chin went up in the air and her face betrayed such a delicate, high-bred disdain that apparently Anthony's fate was immediately settled.

The little party had now reached the familiar pine woods and there, only a few yards ahead, stood their deserted cabin. The totem pole raised its gaunt head to greet them, still decorated with the history of their year in the woods together. But the doors and windows of the cabin were barred with heavy planks. Nowhere was there a sign of life.

"Let's go back home at once, please, now that we have seen that everything is all right," Mollie begged a moment later. "It always gives me the blues dreadfully to see Sunrise Cabin closed up and to know that perhaps no one of us shall ever live there again. I never dreamed when we said good-bye to it last spring that we would not come out here often for club meetings and parties."

"Parties?" Meg repeated. Then she continued standing perfectly still and silent for several moments, although the others were moving about laughing and talking.

"Parties!" she exclaimed again, speaking in such a loud tone that her companions turned to stare at her in surprise.

"Betty Ashton, Mollie O'Neill and Billy Webster, if you and some of the others will help us, why can't we have our dinner party here at the cabin? We are not planning to have it until New Year, so there will be plenty of time to make arrangements."

However, Meg could get no further with her suggestion, for Betty and Mollie had both flung their arms about her and Betty exclaimed:

"It will almost make me have a happy holiday time, Meg dearest, and I can never bear to refuse your invitation if we are to be together at Sunrise Cabin once again."

CHAPTER IX
THE CASTLE OF LIFE

It seemed to Esther Crippen that she had been sitting in the wings of the theater every evening for half her lifetime, although it had been only a week since Polly's initial appearance as the Fairy of the Woods in the dramatization of the ancient legend "The Castle of Life."

At first she had spent every moment after Polly's departure from the dressing room in peering out from some inconspicuous corner at whatever action was taking place upon the stage. Now, however, the play and even the actors themselves had become a comparatively old story. Her interest centered itself chiefly in Polly--in Polly and the odd human characters that she saw everywhere about her. Indeed, except for her nervousness and care of her friend, this week had been almost as absorbing to Esther Crippen as to the other girl. For after the first two nights she had lost her fear that Polly might make an absolute failure of her part, and also the impression that either of them might be insulted or unkindly treated by the men and women about them. People had been rough perhaps, but thoroughly business-like. And if Polly were told to hurry, or to move on, or corrected for some mistake in her work, it was all done in so impersonal a fashion that both girls had learned valuable lessons from the experience. Esther had been amazed at the spirit in which Polly had accepted the discipline and hard work. Perhaps, after all, she had been making a mountain out of a mole hill and this disobedience on Polly's part, wrong though it certainly was, might not result in anything so disastrous as she had at first feared.

And there was no doubt that Polly was achieving a real success, one that surprised her and every one else. Her part was only a small one, with but few words to speak; otherwise she could never have managed it with no previous experience and so little time for rehearsing. Nevertheless she had made one of those sudden yet conspicuous triumphs that are so frequent in stage life. Sometimes it may happen with a girl playing the part of a maid, sometimes with a man who has not half a dozen sentences to recite. It is the quality in the acting that counts. And the manager in choosing Polly for the special role he had desired had chosen wisely. For it was not so much the girl's method of playing that had won sympathy and applause, as her manner and appearance.

And curiously enough, though Polly was frightened the first night of the performance, she was not so much so as on that evening of the Camp Fire play the previous year, before an audience of friends.

Polly felt herself at the heart of her first great adventure. The play itself, the other actors and actresses, the strangeness of her surroundings, all occupied her to the forgetting of her own individuality. It seemed as though she were only living out a kind of dream. Nothing was real, nothing was actual about her. The audience did not terrify her, nor the lights, nor the darkness, nor the queer smell of dust and paint and artificiality, that is a necessary part of the background of stage life.

Perhaps the girl had found her element. For there is for each one of us a place in this world, some niche into which one really fits. And though this place may seem crowded, or ugly, or undesirable to other people, if it should be our own, it holds a feeling of comfort and of possession that no other spot can.

But Polly had not been thinking of niches or elements or anything of the kind either tonight or during the week past. All of her being was too deeply absorbed in the interest of the play and the actors and her own little part.

At the present moment she was in hiding behind a piece of scenery, eagerly awaiting the cue for her own entrance; yet she was as keenly intent upon each detail of the acting taking place upon the stage as if tonight it were a first experience.

The players happened to be the two persons who had been kindest and most helpful to her in the company. And one of them one was the brown-eyed girl whose lead she had followed on the day of her own engagement. Polly had been glad to make the discovery later that this same girl had been engaged to play the part of Grazioso's grandmother in "The Castle of Life." The other actor was the star, a young man of about twenty-six or seven, who was impersonating Grazioso, the hero of the fairy story.

The stage was in semi-darkness, while the grandmother related to the boy the tale of her first meeting with the fairies. A small, shabby room revealed a low fire burning in the grate. In an armchair sat the old woman, while her grandson lay on the floor at her feet with his head resting upon his hand.

"There are two fairies," said the grandmother, "two great fairies--the Fairy of the Water and the Fairy of the Woods. Ten years ago I had gone out at daybreak to catch the crabs asleep in the sand, when I saw a halcyon flying gently towards the shore. The halcyon is a sacred bird, so I never stirred for fear I should scare it away. And at the same time from a cleft in the mountain I saw a beautiful green adder appear and come gliding along the sands toward the bird. When they were near each other the adder twined itself around the neck of the halcyon as if it were embracing it tenderly. Then I saw a great black cat, who could be nothing else than a magician, hiding itself behind a rock close to me. And scarcely had the halcyon and adder embraced than the cat sprang on the innocent pair. This was my time to act. I seized him in spite of his struggles and with the knife I used for opening oysters I cut off the monster's head, paws and tail. And as soon as I had thrown the creature's body into the sea, before me stood two beautiful ladies, one with a crown of white feathers and the other with a scarf made of snake's skins. They were, as I have told you, the Fairy of the Water and the Fairy of the Woods."

With these words, Polly moved a few steps nearer the place set for her entrance. On the opposite side she could see the other girl who impersonated the water fairy, also ready to make her entrance. Tonight was New Year's eve and the house was unusually crowded.

But the grandmother was continuing her speech.

"Enchanted by a wicked Jinn, they were obliged to remain bird and snake until some hand should restore them to liberty. To me they owed freedom and power. 'Ask what thou wilt,' they said, 'and thy wishes shall be fulfilled."

"I thought how I was old and had too hard a life to wish for it over again. But the day would come when nothing would be too good for thee, my child." The old woman leaned over, stroking her grandson's dark hair. "The Fairy of the Woods gave me a scale from the snake's skin and the Fairy of the Water a small white feather from her crown. They are hidden in a box under some rags. Open the box and thou wilt find the scale and the feather."

The boy then crossed the stage and a moment later handed the box to the old woman, who appeared too ill to leave her chair.

After bending over and listening to her instructions, he stepped forward nearer the footlights. There in the center of the room was a bowl of water in which he placed the feather and the scale.

"Wish for thyself anything thou desirest, fortune, greatness, wit, power," murmurs the old woman. "But embrace me first, as I feel that I am dying."

But Grazioso did not approach either to embrace or ask the old woman's blessing.

"I wish my grandmother to live forever!" he cried. "Appear, Fairy of the Woods. Appear, Fairy of the Water!"

And now in perfect silence Polly O'Neill made her entrance. She moved very slowly forward, so slim and young and tall, with such big, dark-blue eyes, and such slender, elfish grace that she did not look like a real flesh-and-blood girl.

The audience stirred, and a little breath of appreciation moved through it, which Polly was almost learning to expect.

She wore her own black hair unbound and hanging loose below her shoulders. It was made blacker by the wreath of leaves that encircled her head. She was dressed in an olive-green gown of some soft, clinging material and a scarf of snake's skin was fastened over her shoulder.

The Fairy of the Water followed Polly. Her gown was white with a blue scarf, and she was small and blonde. She was a pretty girl, but somehow there was no suggestion of the fairy about her. One could see the same type of girl any time, standing behind a counter in a shop, or dancing at a party of young people.

Polly's grace and her ardent, unconventional temperament made it easy to understand why the attention should be focused upon her during this single scene. Besides, she had one long speech to deliver.

This was the moment when the girl felt her only real nervousness. For always there was the uncertainty as to whether her voice would be strong and full enough to be heard throughout the theater. Tonight and for the first time she hesitated for a second. Yet no one noticed it, except the actors near her and Esther, who had crept forth, for a closer view in spite of the stage regulations.

"Have you forgotten your lines, child?" the leading man whispered so quietly that no one could overhear.

But Polly only smiled, with a faint shake of her graceful head.

"Here we are, my child," she began the next instant, speaking in clear, girlish tones that showed nothing of indecision or embarrassment.

"We have heard what you said and your wish does you credit. We can prolong your grandmother's life for some time. But to make her live forever you must find The Castle of Life."

"Madam," replied Grazioso, "I will start at once."

"It is four long days' journey from here," the Fairy of the Woods continued. "If you can accomplish each of these four days' journey without turning out of your road and if, on arriving at the castle, you can answer the three questions that an invisible voice will ask you, you will receive there all that you desire. For there the fountain of immortality will be found."

Then slowly the great stage curtain descended. And this was the end of Polly's part in the performance, though one more ordeal was to follow. And though she welcomed this, Polly also dreaded it more than anything else. Always a curtain call came at the close of this scene, when she and the Fairy of the Water, each holding a hand of Grazioso's, must step forth to the footlights and for an instant face the audience, smiling their thanks for the applause.

But Polly had never been able to summon a smile, for at this moment she had always become self-conscious. The glamour and the excitement of the theater suddenly deserted her and she felt not like a fairy or anything fantastic, but only like Polly O'Neill, a very untrained and frightened girl who was deceiving her family and friends to have this first taste of stage life, and who might suffer almost any kind of consequences: imprisonment in some boarding school, Polly feared, where she might never again be allowed any liberty or an equal imprisonment in Woodford, with no mention of the theater made in her presence as long as she lived. For Polly could not determine to what lengths her mother's anger and disapproval of her conduct might lead her. And she did mean to make her confession and face the results as soon as her two weeks' engagement was over.

Therefore tonight she kept an even tighter clasp on Grazioso's hand than usual, her knees were shaking so absurdly. And all the faces in the audience were swimming before her, as though they had no features but eyes. Then suddenly the girl grew rigid with surprise, uncertainty and fear.

In the second row just under the footlights she had discovered a face that was strangely familiar. And yet could it be possible that this person of all others should be here in New York City and in the theater tonight, instead of in the village of Woodford?

CHAPTER X
THE RECOGNITION

Esther was not waiting in the accustomed place where Polly had previously found her when she came off the stage. On her way to the dressing room she shivered a little, missing the coat that her friend was in the habit of wrapping about her shoulders. The night was extremely cold and the back of a theater is nearly always breezy.

Polly hurried faster than usual to her room--a small dark one at the end of a passage-way. But even here there was no sign of Esther. What could have become of her? She was not apt to be talking with any of the members of the company; for both girls had decided that it was wiser to make themselves as inconspicuous as possible.

Well, she must do her best to get out of her fairy costume and back into sensible garments by her own efforts. Esther would be coming along in a few moments. She could not stand idle with her teeth fairly chattering and those ridiculous little chills chasing themselves all over her. Wouldn't it be too absurd to take cold at this particular time and so make a failure of her adventure? For she would thus heap all the family disapproval and punishment upon her own head and incur the righteous indignation of everybody in the company by having to resign her part.

Would any one ever have imagined that a garment could be so difficult to unfasten as this one she was now incased in? For of course the stiffness and shakiness of Polly's fingers came from the zero temperature in her dressing room and not in the least from the momentary fright she had received from her supposed recognition of a face in the audience. Undoubtedly she had been mistaken. Yet why should she have chosen to believe that she saw about the most unlikely person of her acquaintance? A guilty conscience should have conjured up some ghost who had more right to be present.

Polly finally did succeed in getting into her street clothes without assistance; and though five, ten minutes passed, Esther did not appear in the dressing room. Nor was she anywhere in the hall, since Polly had several times thrust her head out the door to look for her.

Polly was a little uneasy, though assuredly nothing serious could have happened to Esther. Esther had been very good to her during these past days, so staunch and loyal, never reproaching her or arguing once she had become convinced that Polly's mind was made up, and taking such wonderful care of her, guarding her so closely! If ever there came a time when her mother, or Mollie, or Betty should attempt to blame Esther for her part in this escapade, Polly had determined that they should understand the situation in its true light. And some day she might be able to return Esther's allegiance and devotion. For always the opportunity to serve a friend will come if one is sufficiently on the lookout for it.

The moment that she left her dressing room Polly ran directly into Esther, who was hurrying toward her.

"Oh, Polly dear," she said, "I hope you haven't been worried, though I have been uneasy enough about you. Do come back into your room for a moment. There is something I want to tell you that no one else must hear."

Esther looked so excited and nervous that Polly slipped an arm comfortingly about her. "Don't mind if anybody has said anything rude or been horrid, please," she whispered. "You know we promised each other not to take the disagreeable things seriously."

"Oh no, it is nothing like that. It is about you," the older girl explained.

Polly smiled. "The disagreeable things usually are about me." She looked so absurdly young and wilful and charming that Esther felt herself suddenly willing to champion her cause against any opposition. Of course Polly had done wrong, but the mistake had been made and to frustrate her ambition now could do no possible good.

"I don't think you understand, Polly; you can't of course. But Billy Webster was in the audience just now and recognized you. He says that Mollie was afraid there was something the matter and----"

"Billy Webster's opinions are not of the least interest to me. Do let's hurry home, Esther. It is almost ten o'clock and though we can take the street car straight to your door, we have never been out this late before."

"But Billy says he *must* see you. He is waiting outside. He says he means to tell your mother and Mollie what you are doing unless you promise to return home tomorrow. He says that if you won't promise he may telegraph them tonight, so your mother can come and get you tomorrow. I think you had better see him."

Suddenly Polly flung her arms about her friend's neck and began crying like a disappointed child. One never could count on Polly's doing what might be expected of her. She had had the boldness of defy opposition and to act successfully for a week on the professional stage; yet now when she most needed her nerve she was breaking down completely.

"I always have hated that Billy Webster," she sobbed, "from the first moment I saw him. What possible reason or right can he have to come spying on me in this fashion? If he tells mother what I am doing now and does not give me a chance to confess, she will never forgive me. Neither will Mollie nor Betty nor any of the people I care about. Rose and Miss McMurtry will never speak to me. I shall be turned out of our Camp Fire Club. Of course I know I deserve it. But that Billy Webster should be the person to bring about my punishment is too much! Besides, I can't give up my part now. Surely, Esther, you can see that. Acting a week longer won't hurt me any more and----"

"I think we had better see Mr. Webster, anyhow, dear," Esther insisted quietly. "Perhaps we can persuade him not to tell, or else to give you the first opportunity."

Hastily Polly dried her eyes. She looked very white and frail as they went out of the room together.

In a secluded corner not far from the stage door they found Billy Webster waiting for them. His face was pale under his country tan. His blue eyes, that sometimes were charmingly humorous, showed no sign of humor now. If ever there was so youthful a figure of a stern and upright judge, he might well have stood for the model.

Polly struggled bravely to maintain her dignity.

"What is your decision, Miss O'Neill?" he inquired, without wasting any time by an enforced greeting. "I presume Miss Crippen has told you what I have made up my mind to do."

Amiability was one of Esther's dominant traits of character; yet she would have liked to shake Billy Webster until his teeth chattered or suppress him in almost any way. After all, what right had he to take this lofty tone with Polly? He was not a member of her family, not even her friend. Just because he had known all of them in their Camp Fire days in the woods and was devoted to Mrs. Wharton and to Mollie was not a sufficient excuse.

Therefore Polly's unexpected meekness of manner and tone was the more surprising--and dangerous.

"How did you happen to come to New York and to the theater, Billy?" she queried, ignoring his use of the "Miss." Frequently in times past they had called each other by their first names, when good feeling happened to be existing between them.

Instantly Billy looked a little more on the defensive. "I--I had to come to New York on business," he explained sullenly. "And Mollie had been telling me that she was kind of uneasy about you and that she felt there must be some reason you wouldn't give why you did not wish to come home for the holidays."

"So you undertook to play detective and find out?" Polly announced in the cool, even tones that made Billy hot with anger and a sense of injustice.

He was perfectly sure that he was right in his attitude toward her. She had been disobedient and audacious beyond his wildest conception, even of her. And yet she had a skilful fashion of making the other fellow appear in the wrong.

"I told Mollie that I would call on you and Esther," he returned, relapsing into his old-time familiarity. "You see, I told her that I was sure things were quite all right, but I wanted to convince her too. I didn't think you would mind seeing me. I thought you might even be glad to hear about your Woodford friends. So as Mollie gave me your address, I went out to your house at about eight o'clock. The maid told me that you had gone to the theater, told me which one. Of course I just supposed that you had gone to see a show. And that was pretty bad for two young girls! But when I got here and the curtain went up and you came out!--why, Polly, I just couldn't believe it at first, and then I got to thinking of how your mother and Mollie would feel and what might happen!" And Billy's voice shook in a very human and attractive fashion.

Instantly Polly's hand was laid coaxingly on the young man's coat sleeve. "But, Billy, seeing as now I have been and gone and done it already, why, think of me in any way that you please. Only don't tell on me for another week. The play is to last only through the holidays. And I promise on my word of honor to come home as soon as it is over and to tell mother every single thing."

"Word of honor?" Billy repeated slightingly. And of course, though Polly deserved her punishment his inflection was both rude and cruel.

Up to this moment the little party of three persons had been entirely uninterrupted. Now Esther heard some one coming quickly toward them. And turning instantly she understood the impression that this scene might make. The man was the leading actor of the company, Richard Hunt, who in a quiet way had shown an interest and an attitude of protection toward Polly. Now observing a strange young man, and Polly's evident agitation, it was but natural that he should suppose that some one was trying to annoy her.

Esther flung herself into the breach. Not for anything must a scene be permitted to take place! And she could guess at Billy Webster's scornful disregard of a man who was an actor. Billy was a country fellow with little experience of life, and broad-mindedness was not a conspicuous trait of his character.

Esther never knew just exactly how she managed it, but in another moment she had confided the entire story of Polly's audacity to Mr. Hunt, Billy Webster's place in it, and his present intention of bringing retribution upon them. She knew there was but little time for her story; for Mr. Hunt might be compelled to leave them on receiving his curtain call at any moment. In a very surprising and good-humored fashion however he seemed to understand the situation at once.

"I had an idea that Miss O'Neill was new to this business," he said; "or you would both have realized that it is not wise for a girl so young as she is to come to the theater without her mother or some much older woman to look after her. But I believe I can appreciate everybody's point of view in this matter. So why wouldn't it be well to have Miss O'Neill telegraph her mother herself and ask that she come down to New York tomorrow. She could say there was nothing serious, so as not to frighten her. And then of course they could talk things over together and decide what was best without any interference."

But before any answer could follow his suggestion a bell sounded and the older man was obliged to hurry away.

Esther breathed a sigh of relief.

"Dear me, why had not one of us thought of this way out?" she asked. "Surely, Billy, you can't object to allowing Mrs. Wharton to be the judge in this matter?"

Billy nodded. "Of course that is the best plan."

"And you, Polly?"

Polly had begun to cry again. "I want to see my mother right this minute," she confessed. And then, slipping out of the stage door, she left Esther and Billy to follow immediately after her and in silence to escort her safely home.

CHAPTER XI
SUNRISE CABIN AGAIN

It was New Year's night. Sunrise Cabin was no longer an empty and deserted place, but golden lights shone through the windows, making a circle of brightness outside the door.

From the inside came the sound of voices and laughter and music and the clatter of dishes.

Slowly a figure approached the door. It was after seven o'clock and a sharply cold evening with a heavy snow on the ground, so there could be small comfort in loitering. Yet when the figure reached its evident destination, instead of knocking or making an effort to enter, it hesitated, stopped, turned and walked away for a few steps and then came back again. The second time, however, summoning a sudden courage, the arm shot forth, and there was a single rap on the door. The rap was so imperative that in spite of the rival noises inside, the door opened quickly. Then the newcomer entered and for another moment stood hesitating in even greater bewilderment.

The great room seemed to be twinkling with a hundred bayberry candles, sending forth a delicious woodland fragrance. The walls were covered with pine branches and the big fireplace was piled as high with burning fagots and pine cones as safety permitted. A long table standing in the center of the room was beautifully and yet oddly decorated, and upon it dinner was just about to be served.

Resting in the middle of its uncovered surface were three short and slender pine logs of the same general height and size and crossed at the top, while swinging from this trident was a brightly polished copper kettle, piled high tonight with every kind of fruit and with giant clusters of white and purple grapes suspended over its sides. Encircling the centerpiece, made not of real wood of course but of paper bon-

bons, were three groups of logs representing the insignia of the three orders of the Camp Fire, the wood-gatherer's logs having no flame, the fire-maker's a small one, while the torch-bearer's flame of twisted colored paper seemed to glow as though it were in truth of fire. The mats on the table were embroidered in various Camp Fire emblems--a bundle of seven fagots, a single pine tree, or a disk representing the sun. And at either end of the long table three candles had lately been lighted, while standing up around it at their appointed places were about twenty guests, the girls dressed in their ceremonial costumes, the young men as Boy Scouts.

The effect of the entire scene was so brilliant and so unusual that there was small wonder that the latest comer was overwhelmed. He fumbled awkwardly with his hat, cleared his throat, his face so crimsoning with embarrassment that actual tears were forced out of his eyes. And then just as the young man was praying that the earth might open and swallow him up, a girl came forward from the indeterminate mass of persons, who appeared to be swimming in a mist before him, and held out her hand.

"I am so glad to see you, Mr. Graham. Nan and I were beginning to be afraid you would not be able to come," she said cordially. "But you are just in time, as we are only sitting down to the table this very minute."

And Meg Everett then led her final guest down what seemed to him a mile's length of table, placing him between two persons, whom at the moment he did not suppose that he had ever seen. And before he could quite recover his senses there was an unexpected burst of music and then a cheer that filled every inch of the cabin space.

"Wo-he-lo for aye, Wo-he-lo for aye, Wo-he-lo, Wo-he-lo, Wo-he-lo for aye! Wo-he-lo for work, Wo-he-lo for health, Wo-he-lo, Wo-he-lo, Wo-he-lo for Love."

And then with laughter Meg Everett's New Year dinner guests took their places at the table and in the pause Anthony Graham had a chance to pull himself together. To his relief he found that Miss McMurtry was seated on his left side, and at least they were acquaintances. For Miss McMurtry had also come to live in the old Ashton house and often passed the young man on the stairs, nodding good-night or good-morning. Then he had put up some book-shelves for her in her room and moved the furniture to her satisfaction. So, perhaps the Camp Fire party might not be so wretchedly uncomfortable with one person near with whom he might exchange an occasional word.

For just what the young man's emotions were this evening, no one except a person placed in a similar position could understand. Perfectly well did he appreciate that Meg had asked him to her dinner only because of her loyalty and affection for his sister, Nan, as a member of her same Camp Fire Club. The brothers of the other girls had been invited, Jim Meade, Frank Wharton and, of course, John Everett, besides others of his friends. So to have left him out might have been to hurt Nan's feelings. His sister was both proud and sensitive over his efforts to make a better position for himself in the village. Yet should he have taken advantage of Meg's kindness and accepted her invitation? Anthony was by no means certain. This same question had been keeping him awake for several nights and even after having written his hostess that she might expect him to appear he had delayed his approach until the last minute.

Assuredly the other young men would not enjoy his presence. They might be coldly polite, but nothing more could be expected. For no one could be more conscious than Anthony was at this time in his life of the difference between him and other men of his age, who had the advantages of birth and education. Actually he could feel the grime of his own hands as he clutched them nervously together under the table. Not all the scrubbing of the past hour could altogether rid them of the soot and dust that came of making fires and sweeping office floors. And his clothes, although brushed until they were spotless, were worn almost threadbare in places. The very shirt that Nan had washed and ironed for him, had had to have the frayed ends trimmed away from the wrist-bands.

Anthony glanced across the table. There were Nan's dark eyes smiling at him bravely. She did not look in the least ashamed of him. And as for Nan herself why, she was as pretty a Camp Fire girl as any one at the table. Wearing their Council Fire costumes, each girl decorated only with the honor beads which she had won by her own efforts, the poorer maids and the rich ones were equally attractive. For there were none of the differences in toilet which any other kind of entertainment might have revealed.

But Nan was not only smiling at her brother, she was nodding at him and trying to attract his attention. Evidently she wished him to glance away from Miss

McMurtry to his companion on the other side. And Anthony finally did manage to turn shyly half way around.

Then with a sudden feeling almost of happiness he discovered that Betty Ashton was on his right. She did not happen to be looking toward him at the moment, but was talking to John Everett with more animation than he had ever before seen her show.

Betty had no knowledge of Anthony's having been invited to Meg's Camp Fire dinner. His invitation had not come so soon perhaps as the others had received theirs, and afterwards for several days he had had no opportunity for conversation with her. For of course living in Betty's house gave him no right to any pretense of friendship with her.

Yet the moments were passing and she must by this time have become conscious of his presence. Miss McMurtry had called him by name several times and no human being could be entirely oblivious of a person so near, unless under some peculiar stress of emotion.

Anthony felt his former nervousness leaving him. He was no longer blushing; his face had become white and a little stern. So that when Betty finally turned to speak to the young man she had a curious impression that his face was unfamiliar, it wore so different an expression from any that she had ever seen on it before. Betty had been conscious of Anthony's presence from the instant of his taking his place beside her and in failing to recognize him had not deliberately intended being rude or unkind. At first she had been amazed and a little chagrined by his presence, for after what she had said to Meg she had not dreamed of the young man's being included among the guests. Yet this was Meg's entertainment and not hers, and of course she had no right to feel or show offense. Only she and John Everett happened to be having such an interesting talk at the moment of Anthony's appearance, and assuredly John shared her conviction about the newcomer! One could be kind to the young fellow of course, without admitting him within the intimate circle of friendship. And Betty Ashton, although she would never have confessed it, had always been greatly influenced by John Everett's opinions and personality. He was such a big blond giant, older and handsomer and more a man of the world than any other college fellow in Woodford. She was flattered, too, because he had never failed on his return for holidays to show her more attention than any other girl in the village. He might have other friendships outside of his own home; of this she could know nothing, but at the present time this thought only made him the more agreeable. Therefore it was annoying that she might be expected to waste a part of her evening on a young fellow for whom she felt no personal interest, only good will. Betty herself was not conscious of the condescension in her attitude, but why did she find it so difficult to begin a conversation with the newcomer or even to greet him?

Anthony should at least understand that it was exceedingly ill mannered of him to keep staring down into his plate when he must have become aware that she was now ready to talk with him. But what should she say first? Having failed to notice a person's existence for some time makes an ordinary "Good evening" appear a bit ridiculous.

"How do you do, Mr. Graham?" Betty began half shyly, putting more cordiality into her manner than usual in an effort to atone for her former lack of courtesy.

Then for the briefest space Anthony glanced up at her quietly, his grave eyes studying hers, until Betty felt her own eyelids flutter and was grateful for the length of her dark lashes which swept like a cloud before her vision. For actually she was blushing in the most absurd and guilty fashion, as though she had done something for which she should feel ashamed.

"Good evening," Anthony returned, and during the rest of the dinner party he never voluntarily addressed a single remark to her.

Betty need not have been afraid that he might interfere with her opportunity for conversation with John Everett. For although Anthony answered politely any questions that she put to him and listened to whatever she wished to say, the greater part of his time he devoted to talking with Miss McMurtry and to pursuing his own train of thought.

For if the young man had originally been doubtful as to whether it was wise for him to accept Meg Everett's invitation, he was glad now with all his heart. Just what this evening was giving him he had needed. Glancing up and down the table, his own resolution was thereby strengthened. If there had been moments when he had wavered, when it had seemed easier to slip back into his old way of life and to enjoy the companions who were always ready to join hands, he could hereafter recall this experience and Betty's treatment of him, as well as the sight of the other young men guests. Some day there should be another reckoning. These fellows were largely what their fathers had made them; they had birth, schooling, the influences of cultured homes. But out in the big world a man's own grit and will and ability to keep on working in the face of every difficulty counted in the long run. Anthony clenched his teeth, feeling his backbone actually stiffen with the strength of his resolution. Then he had the humor and good sense to laugh at himself and to begin taking more pleasure in his surroundings.

Here were all the Camp Fire girls whom his sister had talked and written so much about, excepting the two whose absence the others were lamenting, Polly and Esther. Here also was the German professor, who had lately moved into the Ashton house, sitting on the further side of Miss McMurtry and certainly absorbing all of her attention that he possibly dared. But Anthony did not mind; he had a kind of fellow feeling for Herr Crippen, who was poor and evidently not of much interest or importance in the Lady Betty's estimation. There at the farther end of the table must be Miss Rose Dyer, the Camp Fire Guardian whom Nan cared for so deeply, and she certainly was quite as pretty as his sister had said. So why should young Dr. Barton be staring at her so severely? Miss Dyer was only laughing and talking idly with Frank Wharton; and every now and then she turned to smile and speak to the little girl who sat close beside her. This must be Faith, the youngest of the Sunrise girls, whose mother had lately died and who was now living with Miss Dyer.

Anthony smiled unexpectedly, so that Betty, who happened to be glancing toward him at the moment, was vexed over his ability to amuse himself. He had only just guessed why Dr. Barton found it necessary to regard Miss Dyer so sternly. Anthony felt that he would like to make friends with this young men. He was evidently somewhat narrow and puritanical, but already had offered to assist him with any of his studies should he need help. And Anthony meant to take advantage of his offer and to interest him if he could; for Dr. Barton was just the kind of a friend he would like to know intimately in these early days of his struggle.

Dinner was finally over, and, stupidly enough, as the guests began leaving the table Anthony Graham felt his own shyness and awkwardness returning. They were intending to dance for the rest of the evening, and dancing was another of the graces that had been left out of his education. However, he could find himself an inconspicuous corner somewhere, and it would be good enough fun to look on.

CHAPTER XII
"LIFE'S LITTLE IRONIES"

Mollie O'Neill, if you don't tell me what you and Billy Webster have been whispering about all evening and why you look so worried, I don't think I can bear it a moment longer," Betty Ashton insisted, having at last found her friend alone for a moment, while the other girls and men were clearing the living room for the dance.

"There isn't anything to tell. At least there really is, but I have not been told just what," Mollie sighed in return.

"Then of course it's Polly?"

Mollie nodded. "Early this morning before any of us were awake a telegram arrived from Polly begging mother to come to New York at once. Polly said she wasn't ill and there was nothing for us to worry over, but just the same Sylvia and I have been worried nearly to death all day. For mother got off within a few hours. Then late this evening Billy Webster appears in Woodford after his visit in New York. And though he tells me that he saw Polly and Esther and has confessed that he knows why Polly telegraphed for mother, he won't give me the least satisfaction about anything. Can you make any suggestion, Betty dear? What difficulty do you suppose Polly has gotten into this time? For certainly it is Polly and not Esther; Esther would never be absurd."

Mollie lowered her voice as several of their friends were approaching.

"Please don't speak of this, Betty. Mother left word that we were not to mention it outside the family until she learned exactly what was the matter. But of course she said that I might tell you."

Before Betty could reply John Everett had invited her to dance.

But slowly she shook her head. "I can't, John. I know you will think it foolish;

perhaps it is. Of course I have come to Meg's party and enjoyed it very much. And yet, well, somehow I don't feel quite like dancing. You understand, don't you?"

John acquiesced. He was disappointed, and yet felt himself able to understand almost anything that Betty wished him to, when she looked at him with that appealing light in her gray eyes and that rose flush in her cheeks.

"Never mind," he returned; "I'll find seats for us somewhere, where we can manage to talk and yet watch the others."

Betty smiled. It was agreeable to be so sought after, and yet under the circumstances quite out of the question.

"You will please find me a place where I can watch, but not with you. This is your party, remember. Meg will expect you and every man to do his duty," she replied.

So after a little further discussion Betty found herself seated upon a kind of miniature throne, which John had made for her by piling some sofa cushions upon an old divan. Behind her was a background of cedar and pine branches decorating the walls and just above her head flickered the lights of candles from a pair of brass sconces.

Betty wore her red brown hair parted in the middle and in two heavy braids, one falling over each shoulder, while around her forehead was a blue and silver band with the three white feathers, the insignia of her title of "Princess" in their Camp Fire Club. Her dress was cut a little low in the throat and about it were strung seven chains of honor beads.

For a little while at least she might have found interest in watching the others dance had she not been worried about Polly. She was uneasy and it was stupid to have been given this opportunity to think; for thinking could do no possible good. Whatever mischief Polly had gotten into was sure to be beyond one's wildest imagination. It would be much more agreeable if she might have some one to talk with her and so distract her attention.

And there was one other guest beside herself who was not dancing. Betty flushed uncomfortably. It must appear strange to the others to see Anthony sitting only a short distance away from her and yet paying no more attention to her presence than if they were upon opposite sides of the world.

Once or twice Betty looked graciously toward the young man, intending to smile an invitation to him to sit near her, should he show the inclination. For possibly he was too much embarrassed to make the first move. She must remember that he had had no one to teach him good manners and that he was always both shy and awkward in her presence.

However, at present he seemed totally unaware of her existence and not in the least requiring entertainment. For he was watching the dancers with such profound concentration that apparently his entire attention was absorbed by them.

The girl had an unusually good opportunity for studying the young man's face. She had not noticed until tonight how thin he was and how clear and finely cut his features. There was no trace of his Italian mother left, save in his black hair and in the curious glow which his skin showed underneath its pallor. His nose was big-- too big, Betty thought--and his lips closed and firm. He had a kind of hungry look. Hungry for what? the girl wondered. Then she had a sudden feeling of compunction. Anthony might sometimes even be hungry for food, he worked so hard, made so little money and was so busy by day and night. Before tonight she might have helped him without his knowing or even caring, if he had guessed her purpose. But after tonight? Well, Betty felt reasonably sure that she and Anthony could never be upon exactly the same footing again. For somehow she had hurt him more than she had intended, not realizing that any one could be at once so humble and so proud. And as she had made one of those mistakes that one can never apologize for, there was no point in dwelling on it any longer. Only she did regret by this time that deep down in her heart there must still linger her old narrow attitude toward money and good birth. She was poor enough herself now, and yet in her case, as in so many others, had it not made her feel all the more pride in the distinction of her family? Assuredly she had often whispered to herself that poverty did not matter when one bore a distinguished name.

Betty smothered a sigh and a yawn. It was tiresome to be sitting there thinking and reproaching herself when the others were having such a good time. How splendidly Billy Webster and Mollie danced together! He was so strong and dictatorial, so certain of his own judgment and opinions. And Mollie so gentle and yielding! She smiled over her foolish romancing, and yet there was no use pretending that they would not make a suitable match should things turn out that way. Mollie and Polly might possibly never be exactly what they had been to each other in the past, and Mrs. Wharton had re-married, and Sylvia would soon be going away to study nursing. But some one was passing close by and trying to attract her attention. Betty waved her hand, but when she had gone frowned a little anxiously.

Edith Norton was dancing with the friend whom she had persuaded Meg to ask to her Camp Fire dinner, although none of the rest of the girls liked him. He was a good deal older than their other young men acquaintances and a stranger to most of them, having only come to Woodford in the past six months and opened a drug store. But he had been entirely devoted to Edith since, and of course as she was nearly twenty she should know her own mind. Notwithstanding, Betty felt uneasy and uncomfortable. They had been hearing things not to Frederick Howard's credit in the village, and Edith had always been unlike the rest of their Sunrise Camp Fire girls. She was vainer and more frivolous and dreadfully tired of working in a millinery shop in Woodford. This much she had confided to Betty after coming to live in the Ashton house. And both Rose Dyer and Miss McMurtry were afraid that Edith might for this reason accept the first opportunity that apparently offered to make life easier for her. So they had asked Betty to use her influence whenever it was possible. Betty it was who had first brought Edith into their club, and Edith had always cared for her and admired her more than any other of her associates.

Betty stirred restlessly. Would she never be able to get away from serious thoughts tonight? But the next instant she had jumped to her feet with a quickly smothered cry and stood with her hands clasped tightly over her eyes. For all around her, in her hair falling down upon her shoulders and about her face were glittering sparks of heat and light. They were scorching her; already she could smell the odor of her burning hair. One movement the girl made to protect her head, then in a flash her hands were covering her eyes again. She wanted to run, and yet some subconscious idea restrained her. Running would only make the flames leap faster and higher. And surely in an instant some one must come to her assistance; for her own low cry had been echoed by a dozen other voices.

Then Betty felt herself roughly seized and dragged stumbling away from her former position, while a sudden, smothering darkness destroyed her breath and vision; and none too tender hands seemed to be pressing down the top of her head.

Another moment and she was pulling feebly at the scorched coat enveloping her.

"Please take it off. I am all right now. The fire must be out, and I'm stifling," she pleaded.

But about her there followed another firm closing in of the heavy material. And then the darkness lifted, showing Anthony Graham standing close beside her in his shabby shirt sleeves, holding his ruined coat in his hands. In a terrified group near by was every other human being in the room, excepting Jim Meade and Frank Wharton, who were pulling down the burning pine and cedar branches from the wall and stamping out the last sparks of fire caused by the overturning of one of the candles.

"What happened to me? Am I much burned?" Betty asked, trying to smile and yet feeling her lips quiver tremulously. "Won't somebody please take me home?" Now she dared not put up her hands toward her pretty hair, for it was enough to try and bear the pain that seemed to be covering her head and shoulders like a blanket of fire. Surely the faces before her must look whiter and more terror-stricken than her own. Mollie and Faith were both crying. Betty wondered just why. And Anthony Graham was staring at her with such a strange expression. She wanted to thank him, to say that she was sorry and grateful at the same time, but could not recall exactly what had happened. Then that funny Herr Crippen was shaking all over and saying "Mein liebes Kind," just as though it were Esther who had been hurt. At last, however, Rose Dyer and Dr. Barton, each with an arm about her, were leading her across the length of that interminable and now pitch-black room with a floor that seemed to be rising before her eyes like the waves of the sea. And afterwards, she did not know just when, the cold night air brought back to her a returning consciousness, but with the consciousness came an even greater sense of pain.

Never in after years could Betty Ashton wholly forget the drive home that followed. Rose Dyer and Miss McMurtry sat on either side of her, sometimes talking, sometimes quiet, and now and then gently touching her bandaged hands. Occasionally Dr. Barton asked her a question, to which she replied as calmly and intelligently as possible. Otherwise she made no movement that she could help and no sound. Anthony Graham drove silently and grimly forward at the utmost speed that the two livery-stable horses could attain. And although to Betty the journey seemed to last half a lifetime, in reality it had seldom been accomplished in so short a time.

CHAPTER XIII
THE INVALIDS

Sylvia Wharton wearing a trained nurse's costume tiptoed into a darkened room.

Instantly the figure upon the bed turned and sighed.

"I don't see why she does not come to me, if she is no worse than you say she is," the voice said. "Really, Sylvia, I think it would be better for you or some one to tell me the truth."

Sylvia hesitated. "She isn't so well, Betty dear. Perhaps Dr. Barton may be angry with me, as he distinctly said that you were not to be worried. But as you are worrying anyhow, possibly talking things over with me may make you feel better. It has all been most unfortunate, Polly's being ill here in your house when you were enduring so much yourself. But it all comes of mother's and everybody's yielding to whatever Polly O'Neill wishes."

Sylvia sat down upon the side of the bed, taking one of Betty's hands in hers. Ten days had passed since the accident at the cabin and the burns on Betty's hands had almost entirely healed, but over her eyes and the upper part of her face was a linen covering, so that it was still impossible to guess the extent of her injury. She was apt to be quieter, however, Sylvia had found out, when she could feel some one touching her. And now the news of Polly for the time being kept her interested.

"You see, mother's first mistake was in not bringing Polly straight back home as soon as she found out what she was doing in New York. Polly had a slight cold then and it kept getting worse each night. But of course Polly pretended that it amounted to nothing and that the stars would fall unless she finished her engagement. So finish it she did, and then hearing of your accident toward the last, as mother and Esther had kept the news a secret from her for some time, why come here she would instead of immediately going home. She wanted to help nurse and amuse you and you had said that you wanted her with you. And then of course Polly was embarrassed over meeting father and Frank. And father was angry at her disobedience and her frightening mother and Mollie. However, that cold of hers has kept on getting worse and she will have to stay in bed now for a few days anyhow. For I won't let Polly O'Neill have her own way this time."

A faint smile showed itself on Betty's lips which Sylvia stooped low enough to see. And then in spite of her own stolid and supposedly cold temperament, the younger girl's expression changed. For it meant a good deal for any one to have succeeded in making Betty Ashton smile in these last few days.

"But you're fonder of Polly than you are of the rest of us, even Mollie, Sylvia, and you let her lead you around," Betty argued.

Sylvia's flaxen head was resolutely shaken. She no longer wore her hair in two tight pigtails, but in almost as closely bound braids wound in a circle about her face. Her complexion was still colorless and her eyes nondescript, but Sylvia's square chin and her resolute expression often made persons take a second look at her. It was seldom that one saw so much character in so young a girl.

"Yes, I am fond of Polly," she agreed, "but you are mistaken if you think I let her influence me. Some one has to take Polly O'Neill sensibly for her own sake." And Sylvia just in time stifled a sigh. For of course her stepsister was in a more serious condition than she had confessed to the other girl. It was well enough to call the illness a bad cold--it was that, but possibly something worse, bronchitis, pneumonia--Dr. Barton had not yet given it a name. She was only to be kept quiet and watched. Later on he would know better what to say. Her constitution was not strong.

Some telepathic message, however, must have passed from one friend to the other, for at this instant Betty sat up suddenly with more energy than she had yet shown.

"If anything dreadful happens to Polly, I shall never forgive Esther as long as I live. It is all very well for Polly and your mother to insist that Esther was not in any possible way responsible. Mollie and I both feel differently. Esther should have told----"

By the fashion in which Sylvia Wharton arose and walked away from the bed,

Betty realized how intensely their opinions disagreed, although the younger girl moved quietly, with no anger or flurry and made no reply.

"Here are some more roses, Betty, that John Everett sent you. Shall I put them near enough your bed to have you enjoy their fragrance?" Sylvia asked. "John seems to be buying up all the flowers near Dartmouth. I told Meg that you would rather he did not send so many. But she says she can't stop him. For somehow John feels kind of responsible for your getting hurt, as he arranged for you to sit under those particular candles. Then he did not notice when you first called for help and let Anthony Graham rescue you. Meg is downstairs now with your mother. Would you like to see her?"

Betty shook her head. "Please don't let Meg know, but I don't feel like talking, somehow. The girls are so sweet and sympathetic. And I try to be brave, but until I know----"

With magically quick footsteps the younger girl had again crossed the room and her firm arms were soon about her friend's shoulders.

"You are going to be all right, dear. Dr. Barton is almost sure of it and I am quite. There won't be any scars that will last and your eyes--why, you protected them marvelously, and they only need resting. You are too beautiful, Betty dear, to have anything happen that could in any way mar you. I can't, I won't believe it."

And somehow Sylvia was one of those people in whose judgment and faith one must always find healing. Betty said nothing more, only put out her hand with an appealing gesture and caught hold of Sylvia's dress.

"I don't want to talk or to see people, and I'm tired of being read to. What is there for me to do, Sylvia child, to make the hours pass?"

Rather desperately the younger girl looked about the great, sunshiny room. It was not Betty's old blue room, but the room once used as a store-room and afterwards occupied by Esther, into which Betty had moved a short while before her accident. Imagination was not Sylvia Wharton's strong point. She was an excellent nurse, quiet, firm and patient and always to be relied upon. But what to do to make Betty Ashton stop thinking of what might await her at the end of her weeks of suffering must have taxed a far more fertile brain than Sylvia's. However, the suggestion did not have to come from her; for at this instant there was a knock at the door, so gentle that it was difficult to be sure that it really was a knock.

Outside stood the German professor with his violin under his arm. And he looked so utterly wretched and uneasy that Sylvia wondered how he could feel so great an emotion over Betty, although the entire village seemed to be worrying as though in reality she had been their own "Princess." No one could talk of anything else until her condition became finally known; but Herr Crippen was a newcomer and Betty had never cared for him.

"Would the little *Fraeulein* like it that I should play for her?" he now asked gently.

And Sylvia turned to the girl on the bed.

At first Betty had shaken her head, but now she evidently changed her mind.

"You are very kind. I think I should enjoy it," she answered. And a few moments afterwards Sylvia stole away.

So there was no one in the room to notice how frequently Herr Crippen had to wipe his glasses as he looked down upon the girl of whose face he could see nothing now save the delicately rounded chin and full red lips.

Then without worrying her he began to play: in the beginning not Beethoven nor Mozart, nor any of the classic music he most loved, but the Camp Fire songs, which he had lately arranged for the violin because of his interest in the Sunrise Hill Camp Fire girls, and which he was playing for the first time before an audience.

And Betty listened silently, not voicing her surprise. The song of "The Soul's Desire," what memories it brought back of Esther and their first meeting in this room! No wonder that Esther had so great talent with such a queer, gifted father. Betty wondered idly what the mother could have been like. She was an American and beautiful, so much she remembered having been told.

Then ceasing to think of Esther she began thinking of herself. Could she ever again even try to follow the Law of the Camp Fire, which had meant so much to her in the past few years, if this dreadful tragedy which hovered over her, sleeping or waking, should be not just a terrible fear, but a living fact. Should she be scarred from her accident, or worse fear, should her eyes be affected by the scorching heat of the flames?

Softly under her breath, even while listening with all her soul to the music, Betty repeated the Camp Fire Law.

"Seek Beauty?" Could she find it, having lost her own? Then she remembered that the beauty which the Camp Fire taught was not only a physical beauty, but the greater kind which is of the spirit as well as of the flesh.

"Give Service?" Well, perhaps some day in ways she could not now imagine, she might be able to return a small measure of the service that her friends had been so generously bestowing upon her.

"Pursue Knowledge, Be Trustworthy." No misfortune need separate a girl from these ideals.

"Hold on to Health." This might mean a harder fight than she had ever yet had to make before, but Betty felt a new courage faintly struggling within her.

"Glorify Work." That was not an impossible demand of her as a Torch Bearer among her group of Camp Fire girls. It was the last of the seven points of their great law that she dreaded to face at this moment, here in the darkness alone.

"Be Happy." Could she ever again be happy even for a day or an hour? And yet the law said: "If we have pain, to hide it, if others have sorrow, be quick to relieve it."

But what the rest of the law read she could not now recall. For Herr Crippen was beginning to play one of the most exquisite pieces of music that can ever be rendered on the violin, Schubert's Serenade.

  "Last night the nightingale woke me,
Last night when all was still
It sang in the golden moonlight"

Betty wondered why the music should sound so strangely far away, as though she were dreaming and it were coming to her somewhere out of the land of dreams.

Another moment and Betty was sound asleep. Nevertheless the Professor, with his eyes still upon her, played softly on, played until Mrs. Ashton noiselessly entered the room.

Then he ceased and the man and woman, standing one on either side of Betty's bed, looked at each other with expressions it would be difficult to translate. For each face held a certain amount of pleading and of defiance.

"She is like her mother; *nicht wahr*?" the Professor murmured, and then withdrew.

Afterwards for several moments Mrs. Ashton's eyes never ceased regarding the curls of Betty's red brown hair, that lay outside on her pillow. Her long braids had been cut off and latterly she had been wearing a little blue silk cap, which had now slipped off on account of her restlessness.

Mrs. Ashton, glancing in a mirror at her own faded flaxen hair, sighed. Then, seating herself in a chair near by she waited in absolute patience and quietness, until suddenly from a movement upon the bed she guessed that Betty was waking.

And actually her child's lips were smiling upon her not only bravely but cheerfully, as though her sleep had brought both comfort and faith.

"Sit close by me, mother," Betty said, "and don't let any one else come in for a long time. You know I have been trying to get you to tell me the history of this old room for ages and now this is such a splendid comfy chance. I am just exactly in the mood for hearing a long, thrilling story."

CHAPTER XIV
"WHICH COMES LIKE A BENEDICTION"

T ell me exactly what you think, Dr. Barton, please, and don't try to deceive me," Betty Ashton pleaded. "I want to be told the truth at once before mother or any one else joins us. Always I shall be grateful to Rose for suggesting that you come here to me alone and when no one was expecting you, so that there need be no unnecessary suspense."

Betty Ashton was seated in a low rocking chair one morning a few days later, with Dr. Barton standing near and carefully unwrapping the bandages from about her head. The room was not brightly lighted, neither was it dark, for a single blind had been drawn up at the window on the opposite side of the room.

Dr. Barton's face showed lines of anxiety and sympathy. Indeed, Rose Dyer could hardly have been persuaded to believe how nervous and shaken he appeared and how, instead of his usual look of hardness and austerity, he was now as tender and gentle as a woman.

"But my dear Betty," he returned in a more cheerful voice than his expression indicated, "what I say to you about yourself is by no means the last word. My opinion, you must remember, is of blessedly little importance. If there are any scars left by my treatment of your burns, there are hundreds of wonderful big doctors who can perform miracles for you. And then time is the eternal healer."

"Yes, I know," the girl answered, "but just the same, please hurry and let me know what you yourself honestly think. At least, I shall be able to tell myself whether my eyes are injured, as soon as you let me try them in a bright light."

For a fraction of a moment Dr. Barton delayed his work. "Won't you allow me to call your mother, or Miss Dyer or Miss McMurtry? Miss Dyer is in the house. I happen to have seen her. And it may be better, in case you do not feel yourself, to have some one else here to care for you. There is Sylvia. Actually I believe she has been of as much use to you and Polly O'Neill as your professional nurses."

At this instant, although she had set her lips so close together that only a pale line showed, Betty's chin quivered, and although her hands gripped the sides of her chair so hard that her arms ached, her shoulders shook.

If only Dr. Barton would cease his perfectly futile efforts to distract her attention. Could any human being think of another subject or person at a time like this?

And Dr. Barton did recognize the clumsiness of his own efforts, only his conversation was partly intended to conceal his own anxiety.

"Don't I hear some one coming along the hall? Are you sure you locked the door?" Betty queried uneasily.

Dr. Barton did not reply. At this instant, although the linen covering still concealed his patient's eyes, he had removed the upper bandages, so that now her forehead was plainly revealed to his view.

And Betty Ashton's forehead had always been singularly beautiful in the past, low and broad with the hair growing in a soft fringe about it and coming down into a peak in the center. Now, however, across her forehead there showed a long crimson line, almost like the mark from the blow of a whip. Dr. Barton examined it closely, touched it gently with the tips of his fingers and then cleared his throat and attempted to speak. But apparently the needed words would not come. On either side the ugly scar the girl's skin was white and fine as delicate silk and on top of her head, which had been protected by her heavy hair, the burns had almost completely healed.

"It is all right, Miss Betty," Dr. Barton said in a curiously husky voice. "You are better than I even dared hope. There is a scar now, but I can promise you that it will be only a faint line in the future, or else will disappear altogether. The very fact that the trouble has concentrated into the one scar shows that the healing has taken place all about it."

Betty's own hands slipped the final covering from about her eyes. Then for a moment her heart seemed absolutely to have stopped beating. For the room swam around her in a kind of disordered dimness. She could see nothing clearly. In a panic she sprang to her feet, when Dr. Barton took a firm hold on her shaking shoulders.

"Be quiet, child. Pull yourself together for just a minute. You are frightened now, you know. In another moment things will clear up and grow more distinct."

And even before he had finished speaking Betty realized this to be the blessed truth.

There in the far end of the big room stood her bed and, on a table near, a bunch of John's pink roses. She could even see their bright color vividly. In another direction was her dressing table and about it hung the photographs of Rose, of Miss McMurtry, of the eleven Camp Fire girls.

Dropping back into her chair Betty, covering her face with her hands, began to sob. And she cried on without any effort at self-control until she was limp and exhausted, although all the while her heart was saying its own special hymn of thanksgiving. And young Dr. Barton kept patting her upon the shoulder and urging her not to cry, because now there was nothing to cry about, until Betty would like to have laughed if the tears had not been bringing her a greater relief. How like a man not to understand that she could now permit herself the indulgence of tears, when for the past two weeks she had not dared, fearing that once having given way there would be no end.

"Would you mind leaving me for a few minutes and trying to find mother?" Betty at last managed to ask.

She wanted to be alone. But a few seconds after the doctor's disappearance, Betty got up and with trembling knees managed to cross her room, feeling dreadfully weak and exhausted from the long suspense. For she wished to look into a mirror with no one watching. And as Betty Ashton got the first glimpse of herself, although vanity had never been one of her weaknesses, she honestly believed that she never had seen any one look so tragically ugly before in her entire life. She hardly recognized herself. Her face was white and thin, almost bloodless except for the scar upon her forehead. Then her hair had been cut off, and though in some places the curls still remained heavy and thick, in others she looked like a badly shorn lamb.

And this time the tears crowding Betty's eyes were not of relief but of wounded vanity.

"I never saw any one so hideous in my life," she remarked aloud. "And I am truly sorry for the people who must have the misfortune of looking at me."

Betty was wearing an Empire blue dressing gown and slippers and stockings of the same color. Her eyes were dark gray and misty with shadows under them. She looked ill, of course, and unlike her usual self, and yet it would be difficult for any misfortune to have made Betty Ashton actually ugly. For beauty is one of the most difficult things in the world to define and one of the easiest to see--a possession that is at once tangible and intangible. And Betty possessed the gift in a remarkable degree.

Therefore she did not look unattractive to the eyes of the young man who was now staring at her in astonishment, fear and delight, from her own open doorway, which Dr. Barton, on leaving the room, had neglected to close.

"I am sorry. Oh, I am so glad!"

Anthony Graham murmured. "I was passing your room; I didn't mean to intrude. But nothing matters now you are well again and looking like yourself. It's so wonderful, so splendid, so----" And the young man, who was ordinarily quiet and reserved, fairly stammered with the rush of his own words.

Betty walked shyly toward him with her eyes still filled with tears.

"Oh, I am dreadful to look at, but I must not complain," she answered wistfully. "A Camp Fire girl ought to have learned some lessons in bravery and endurance. Please let's don't talk about me. I want to thank you, for if it had not been for you, I might have--I can't bear to think even now what might have happened to me."

"Then don't," the young man returned brusquely, but Betty did not this time misunderstand his manner. "I did not do anything. I ought to have gotten to you sooner. I have been hating myself ever since for the time I took to reach you. After all you had done for me in the past!"

The next moment the girl put her hand into the boy's hard, work-roughened one. "Ask Nan to tell the others for me. And remember that no matter what has happened or may happen in the future, I shall always feel myself in your debt, not you in mine."

CHAPTER XV
SECRETS

It was sundown. The big Ashton house, although so filled with people, was oddly quiet. Betty Ashton slipped out of her own room into the hall and hurried along the empty corridor. Once only she stopped and smiled, partly from amusement and partly from satisfaction. Herr Crippen's door was half open and so was Miss McMurtry's and the Professor was playing on his violin. Such sentimental love ditties! The air throbbed with German love songs.

And Betty had a mischievous desire to stick her head into Miss McMurtry's room and see if she was engaged in some maiden-like occupation, such as marking school papers or reading the **Woodford Gazette**. Or was she sitting, as she should be, with her hands idly folded in her lap and her heart and mind absorbed in the music? Never had Betty given up her idea that a romance was in the making between their first Camp Fire guardian and Esther's father. And often since their coming to live in her house had she not seen slight but convincing evidences? Why should Donna so often appear with a single white rose pinned to her dress or take to playing the same tunes on the piano that the Professor played on his violin, particularly when she was an exceedingly poor pianist?

Nevertheless it was not awe of her teacher and guardian that kept Betty from investigating the state of her emotions at this moment; neither was it any fear of antagonism between them, for since Esther's departure to study in New York, Miss McMurtry apparently felt more affection for Betty than for any of the other Camp Fire girls. No, it was simply because she had a very definite purpose which she wished to accomplish without interruption or opposition.

The next instant and she had paused outside a closed door and stood listening tensely. There were no noises inside, no voices, nor the stir of any person moving about. Betty put her hand on the knob and opened it silently.

Instantly there was a little cry and Betty and Polly O'Neill were in each other's arms.

"Betty, you darling," Polly gasped, "turn on every light in this room and let me stare and stare at you. There isn't anything in the world the matter with you. You are as lovely as you ever were. Oh, I have been so frightened! I have not believed what anybody told me, and it seemed it must be a part of my punishment that you had been injured. It is absurd of me, I suppose, but I have had a kind of feeling that perhaps if I had been at Meg's party I should have been with you at the time so that it couldn't have happened."

"Foolish Polly! But when was Polly anything but foolish?" the other girl returned, taking off her cap and pushing back her hair. "You see I am a sight, dear, but it does not matter a great deal. I am kind of getting used to myself these last few days. So I didn't see any reason why, since you are better and I am perfectly well, we could not be together. Even if it does give you a kind of a shock to look at me, you'll get over it, won't you?"

In reply Polly had one of her rather rare outbursts of affection. She was never so demonstrative as the other girls. Her devotions had ways of expressing themselves in an occasional compliment tendered perhaps in some whimsical, backhanded fashion, or in a fleeting caress, which came and was gone like the touch of a butterfly's wing.

Now, however, she took her friend's face between her two hands and kissed her quietly, almost solemnly upon the line of her injury.

"Never say a thing like that to me again as long as you live, Betty Ashton. Perhaps I haven't as much affection as other people. Mother and Mollie are both insisting it lately. Still I know that----but how silly we are to talk of it! You are not changed. Of course I am sorry that your hair had to be cut off, but it will grow out again and the scar will disappear. I wish I could get rid of my"--Polly hesitated--"blemishes so easily," she finished.

Betty looked puzzled. "What do you mean? Sylvia says you are very much better and that there is no reason why you should not get up. She declares that it is only that you won't and that she does not intend nursing you or letting any one else take care of you after a few days, unless you do what Dr. Barton tells you. Sylvia is a dreadfully firm person. She was quite angry with me when I said that I did not believe you were well and that I was quite strong enough now to take care of you and you should not get out of bed until you had entirely recovered."

"But I have entirely recovered and I am well and somehow I can't manage to deceive Sylvia Wharton no matter how hard I try," Polly announced in a half-amused and half-annoyed manner.

"Then why are you trying to?" Betty naturally queried. Of course one never actually expected to understand Polly O'Neill's whims, but now and then one of them appeared a trifle more mysterious than the others. "If you are still tired and feel you prefer to remain in bed, that is a sure sign you are not strong enough to get up, and Dr. Barton and Sylvia ought to realize it," she continued, still on the defensive.

But Polly only smiled at her. "But, dear, I don't prefer to remain in bed. I am so deadly bored with it that as soon as I am left alone I get up and dance in the middle of the floor just to have a little relief. Can't you and mother and Mollie understand (I don't believe any one does except Sylvia) that I don't want to get up because I don't want to have to face the music?"

Still the other girl looked puzzled.

"Can't you see that as long as I have been able to be sick nobody has dared to say very much to me about my escapade in New York? Oh, of course I know what they think and mother did manage to say a good deal before we came home; still, there is a great deal more retribution awaiting me. In the first place, I shall have to go home to the Wharton house. I realize it has been dreadful, my being sick here, but I am everlastingly grateful to you and your mother. Mr. Wharton won't say anything much; he really is very kind to me; but naturally I know what he thinks. And then when Frank Wharton is there it will be so much worse. You see, Frank and I quarreled once, because I thought he was rude to mother. And of course he considers my disobedience worse than his rudeness. And as he is perfectly right, I can't imagine how I shall answer him back the next time we argue."

As Polly talked she had risen into a sitting posture in bed and was now leaning her chin on her hand in a characteristic attitude and quite unconscious of the amusing side to her argument until Betty laughed.

Polly had on a scarlet flannel dressing sacque and her hair was tied with scarlet ribbons. And indeed her cheeks were almost equally vivid in color.

"But there isn't anything funny about my punishment, Betty dear. And the worst of it is that I know I deserve all of it and more and shan't ever have the right to complain. Mother declares that she does not expect to allow me to leave Woodford again until I am twenty-one, since she has no more faith in me. And then, and then--" Polly's entire face now changed expression--"has any one told you that my behavior is to be openly discussed at the next meeting of our Camp Fire Club? Perhaps I won't be allowed to be a member any longer."

Instantly Betty jumped up from her kneeling position by the bed and commenced walking up and down the length of the room, saying nothing at first, but with her lips set in obstinate lines.

"But it isn't the custom of Camp Fire clubs to act as both judge and jury, is it, Polly?" she inquired. "At least, I have never heard of any other club's undertaking such a task. We are allowed, I know, to be fairly free in what we do in our individual clubs, but somehow this action seems unkind and dangerous. For if once we begin criticising one another's faults or mistakes, after a while there won't be any club. Right now Edith Norton is behaving very foolishly, I think, but I wouldn't dream of even discussing her with you or any one of the girls. I----" Betty paused to get her breath, her indignation and opposition to Polly's information overwhelming her.

But Polly held out both hands, entreating her to sit beside her again.

"You are mistaken. I did not explain the circumstances to you as I should have. It is all my idea and my plan to have the girls consider my misconduct and find out how they feel about me," Polly explained quietly. "I spoke of it first to Rose and then to Miss McMurtry and at first they thought in a measure as you do. But I don't agree with you. You remember that our honor beads come to us for obedience and service to our Camp Fire laws. Why should not disobedience make us unworthy to wear them? In the old days if an Indian offended against the laws of his tribe he was made to suffer the penalty. And I don't want you girls to keep me in our club just because you are sorry for me and are too kind to be just. Mollie has told me how horrified Meg and Eleanor and Nan are, and of course Rose and Donna have not pretended to hide their disapproval, even during their consolation visits to me as an invalid. But you will forgive me, won't you, Betty?" Polly ended with more penitence than she had yet shown to any one save her mother.

"Of course I forgive you. But if you had not gotten well I should never have forgiven Esther," the other girl answered.

Two fingers were laid quickly across Betty Ashton's lips.

"Don't be unfair and absurd," Polly protested; "for some day you may be sorry if you don't understand just how big and generous Esther Crippen is. It isn't only that she would sacrifice her own desires for other people's, but that she actually has. I would not be surprised if Esther did not have some secret or other." And Polly stopped suddenly, biting her tongue. Not for worlds would she even in the slightest fashion betray a suspicion or inference of her own concerning the friend who had been so loyal and devoted to her.

Fortunately Betty was too intent upon her own thoughts to have heard her.

"I have to go back to my own room now, but you are not to worry, Polly mine, not about anything. In the first place, you are not to go home very soon. I have talked to your mother and mine and persuaded them that I need to have you stay on here with me. I do need you, Polly. It is queer, but I want you to come and sleep in the old back room with me. I have gotten nervous being in there by myself. There is a mystery about the room greater than I have dreamed. I have only been joking half the time when I have spoken of it. But the other day I got mother to the point where there was no possible excuse for her not explaining the entire reason for her attitude and Dick's toward the place, when suddenly she broke down and left me. We might amuse ourselves while we are invalids discovering whether or not it is haunted. Only I don't exactly wish to make the discovery alone."

CHAPTER XVI
THE LAW OF THE FIRE

Mollie O'Neill walked slowly toward the Ashton house one afternoon not long afterwards at about four o'clock, looking unusually serious and uncomfortable. She was wearing a long coat buttoned up to her chin and coming down to the bottom of her dress, and was carrying a big book.

"Mollie, there isn't anything the matter? Neither Betty nor Polly is worse again?" Billy Webster inquired, unexpectedly striding across from the opposite side of the street and not stopping to offer his greeting before beginning his questioning.

Mollie shook her head, although her face still retained so solemn an expression that the young man was plainly alarmed. Ordinarily Mollie's blue eyes were as untroubled as blue lakes and her forehead and mouth as free from the lines of care or even annoyance.

Billy Webster put the book under his arm and continued walking along beside her.

"If there is anything that troubles you, Mollie, and you believe that I can help you, please don't ever fail to call on me," he suggested in the gentle tones that he seemed ever to reserve for this girl alone. "I know that Polly is dreadfully angry over my interference in New York, but so long as you and your mother thought I did right and were grateful to me, I don't care how Polly feels--at least, I don't care a great deal. And I believe I should behave in exactly the same way if I had it all to do over again."

Shyly and yet with an admiration that she did not attempt to conceal Mollie glanced up at her companion. Billy was always so determined, so sure of his own ideas of right and wrong, that once having made a decision or taken a step, he never appeared to regret it afterwards. And this attitude under the present circumstances was a consolation to Mollie. For oftentimes since Polly's return and while enduring her reproaches, she had experienced twinges of conscience for having concerned an outsider in their family affairs, though somehow Billy did not seem like an outsider. Polly had insisted that she had been most unwise in asking him to look up Esther and herself immediately upon his arrival in New York. How much better had she waited and let Polly make her confession to their mother later, thus saving all of them excitement and strain! However, since Billy was still convinced that he would do the same thing over again in a similar position, Mollie felt her own uncertainty vanish.

"No, there isn't anything you can help about this afternoon," she replied. "I am only going to a monthly meeting of our Council Fire. The girls told me that if I liked I need not come, yet it seems almost cowardly to stay away. For you see Polly has insisted that we talk over her conduct and decide whether or not we wish her to remain a member of our club. Or at least whether some of her honor beads should be taken from her and her rank reduced. There is a good deal of difference of opinion. For some of the girls are convinced that once our honor beads are lawfully won, nothing and no one has the right to take them from us; while others feel that breaking the law of the Camp Fire should render one unworthy of a high position in the Council and that even though one is not asked to resign, at least one should be relegated to the ranks again. But of course all this is a secret and must never be spoken of except in our club."

"Like an officer stripped of his epaulettes," Billy murmured. And afterwards: "See here, Mollie, if this is a club secret then you ought not to have told me and I ought not to have listened. For it is pretty rough on Polly. But I promise not to mention it and will try to forget. We must not make her any more down upon me than she is already."

The young man and girl had now come to the Ashton front gate, and as they stopped, Billy gave the book to Mollie and could not forbear patting her encouragingly upon the coat sleeve. She looked so gentle and worried. Polly always seemed to be getting her into hot water without really intending that Mollie should be made to suffer.

"It will turn out all right, I am sure," he insisted in a convincing tone. "Your sister will always have too many friends to let things go much against her in this world."

Mollie found that the other girls had already assembled in the Ashton drawing room and, as she was late, the camp fire had been laid and lighted, following the same ceremony as if it had taken place outdoors.

The members were all present excepting Polly, who had declined coming down to make her own defense, and Esther, who was still at work in New York. The two Field girls, Juliet and Beatrice, completed the original number, as they were both in Woodford for the winter attending the High School. Rose Dyer, with Faith's hand tight in hers, appeared uneasy and distressed. In her role of Camp Fire Guardian she was not assured of the wisdom of their proceedings and could find no precedent for it among other Camp Fire clubs. However, Miss McMurtry had consented to join their meeting and, as she had been the original and was now the head Guardian of all the clubs in Woodford, the responsibility might honestly be shared with her.

For the first time since her accident Betty Ashton was able to attend a gathering of the Council Fire; and although she was the center of the greater part of the attention and affection in the room, Betty appeared as nervous and worried as Mollie O'Neill.

To both of the girls this open discussion of one of their club member's misdeeds was abhorrent. And that the accused should be their adored but often misguided Polly made the situation the more tragic and distasteful.

Although she was not yet in a position to be positive, Betty felt reasonably convinced that Edith Norton was at the bottom of this formal judgment of Polly. So skilfully and quietly had the older girl gone to work that both Rose Dyer and Miss McMurtry were under the impression that the original suggestion had come from the culprit herself.

Yet the truth was that Edith Norton had a smaller nature than any other member of the Sunrise Hill Camp Fire Club and she and Polly had never been real friends since the night long ago of the Indian "Maiden's Feast," when Edith thinking to fix the guilt of a theft upon Nan Graham, had wakened Polly to a sudden sense of her own responsibility. And it was following a visit of condolence to Polly's sick room by Edith that swift as a flash Polly had announced herself as willing and ready to have her conduct considered by the club council. For it afterwards appeared that Edith had casually mentioned that the other girls had been talking among themselves of this question of Polly's fitness or unfitness to continue a "Torch Bearer" in the club. So with her usual recklessness and impulsiveness she had insisted that her offense be openly considered and that she receive whatever punishment might be considered just. Never had she planned denying her misdeed nor taking refuge behind her friends' affection.

Therefore both Betty and Mollie had been entreated, even ordered, to listen quietly to whatever might be said of her behavior and without protest. And Mollie had agreed. Betty had reserved the right to use her own discretion and had no intention of not making herself felt when the moment arrived.

After the regular business of the meeting had been concluded a marked silence followed, the girls hardly daring even to glance toward one another.

Rose Dyer coughed nervously, yet as she had been chosen to set Polly's case plainly before the other girls and to ask for their frank opinions of what action, if any, the Sunrise Hill Club desired to take, her responsibility must not be evaded. Of course all of the girls had previously heard the entire story, but perhaps in a more or less highly colored fashion. And particularly Polly O'Neill insisted that Esther Crippen's part in her action be explained. For Esther must not be held in any way accountable, as both Betty and Mollie had been inclined to feel.

When Rose had finished a simple statement of the facts of the case and had asked to hear from the other club members, no one answered. Betty kept her eyes severely fastened upon Edith Norton's face. Surely Edith must be aware of her knowledge of certain facts that were as much to her discredit as Polly's disobedience. Of course nothing could induce her to make capital of this knowledge, since Betty Ashton's interpretation of Camp Fire loyalty was of a different kind from Edith Norton's, as the older girl was one day to find out. Nevertheless there was nothing to prevent Betty from using her influence with the hope that Edith might be discouraged from making any suggestion that would start the tide of feeling rolling against the culprit.

This Council Meeting might be a greater test of the entire Camp Fire organization than any one of the girls realized. Possibly it had been a mistake to allow the fitness or unfitness of a fellow member to be openly discussed; especially when the girl was Polly O'Neill, for Polly was a powerful influence always and the club might easily split upon a criticism of her. Whatever should happen, however, Betty Ashton intended using every effort to keep the Sunrise Hill Camp together, saving Polly also if she could.

In spite of her friend's restraining glance, Edith apparently failed to regard her, for instead she glanced insinuatingly toward Eleanor Meade and Meg Everett. Both these girls had expressed themselves as deeply shocked and grieved over Polly's behavior, though neither of them appeared to be ready to make any statement of their views on this occasion. It was one thing to express an informal opinion of another girl's action, but quite another to make a formal accusation against her in the club where they had lived and worked and grown together in bonds almost closer than family ones.

Next Edith studied Sylvia Wharton's expression. Day and night had Sylvia nursed Polly with infinite patience, and yet she had made no effort to conceal her disapproval of her stepsister's conduct and Sylvia might always be relied upon for an honest and straightforward statement of her opinion. Yet Sylvia's face at the present moment was as empty as though she had never had an idea in her life.

Just why this continuing silence should make the original Sunrise Hill Camp Fire guardian smile, no one understood. However, the Lady of the Hill knew very well why and was feeling strangely relieved. For had she not permitted a dangerous test of the Camp Fire spirit to be tried and were the girls not responding just as she had hoped and believed they would? Surely during these past two years they had been developing a real understanding of comradeship, the ability to stick together, to keep step. And girls and women had for so many centuries been accused of the inability to do this.

"I think that no one of us holds Esther Crippen in any way responsible for Polly O'Neill's action or for continuing to keep her family in ignorance of what she was doing," Edith finally began in a rather weak voice, seeing that no one else showed any sign of speaking. "It is one of the things that I think she is most to be blamed for, since it is hardly fair to bring another club member into a difficulty on account of her feeling of personal loyalty."

Betty frowned. There was so much of truth in Edith's speech that it could hardly fail to carry a certain amount of conviction.

But before any one could reply, Sylvia Wharton got up from the floor, where she had been sitting in Camp Fire fashion, and crossing the room, stood before the flames, facing the circle of girls with her hands clasped in front of her and her lips shut tight together. Her usually sallow skin was a good deal flushed.

"I am going to make a motion to this club," she announced, "but before I do I want to say something, and everybody knows how hard it is for me to talk. I can do things sometimes, but I can't say them. Just now Edith Norton used the word, 'loyalty.' I am glad she did, because it is just what I want to speak of--because it seems to me that loyalty is the very foundation stone of all our Camp Fires. Of course Polly has broken a part of our law. She has failed to be trustworthy, but I am not going into that, since each one of you can have your own opinion of her behavior and would have it anyway no matter what I said. But the whole point is, won't every single girl in the Sunrise Hill Camp Fire Club possibly break some of the rules some day? As we are only human, I think we are pretty sure to. So I move that we say nothing more about Polly. Perhaps others of us have done things nearly as bad or will do them. But more important and what I would so much like to persuade you to feel about as I feel is this:"--and Sylvia's plain face worked with the strength of an emotion which few people had ever seen her display before--"I want us to promise ourselves and one another that no matter what any fellow member of the Sunrise Hill Camp Fire Club ever does, or what mistake she may make, or even what sin she may commit, that no one of us will ever turn her back upon her or fail to do anything and everything in our power to help her and to make things happy and comfortable again. I wish I could talk like Betty and Polly, but you do understand what I mean," Sylvia concluded with tears compounded of embarrassment and earnestness standing in her light blue eyes.

"Hear, hear!" whispered Miss McMurtry a little uncertainly.

Rose Dyer clapped her hands softly together. The sound gave the necessary suggestion to the other girls, and poor Sylvia crept back to her place in the circle in a storm of applause. It was the simplest method by which the girls could reveal their deeper emotions. A few moments afterward Sylvia's proposal was put into the form of a regular motion and carried without a dissenting voice.

CHAPTER XVII
A FIGURE IN THE NIGHT

Polly," a muffled voice murmured in so low a tone that the sound was scarcely audible. Then a cold hand was slid beneath the bed clothes, clasping a warm, relaxed one and pressing it with sudden intensity.

"Betty, did you call me?" Polly O'Neill inquired, turning over sleepily and trying to pierce the darkness so as to get a view of her companion. Now that she was coming to her senses, she could feel Betty's body straining close up against her own and her lips almost touching her ear.

It was between two and three o'clock in the morning and the two friends had been sleeping together in Betty Ashton's old-fashioned four-post bed, hung with blue curtains that opened only for a space of several feet in the center of the two sides. The room was dark and cold, for there was no light burning and the sky outside held the blackness that often precedes the dawn. A window was open, letting in sudden gusts of freezing air.

"You aren't ill, are you?" Polly was about to ask when the other girl's fingers closed over her mouth.

"Don't speak and don't stir," Betty whispered, still in almost noiseless tones. "Just listen for a moment. Try and not be frightened, but do you think you can hear any one moving about in this room?"

For the first instant Polly felt a decided inclination to laugh. What an absurd suggestion Betty was making! She must have been asleep and dreamed something that had frightened her. It was rather to be expected, however, after the shock of her accident at the cabin. Therefore it would be best to gratify her fancy; and Polly set herself to listening dutifully.

Then Polly herself started, only to feel once more the other girl's restraining clasp. But the sound she had heard was only the banging of the blind against the window. Nevertheless with the quick Irish sensitiveness to impressions, to subtle suggestions, she was beginning to have a terrifying consciousness of some other person in their bedroom than herself and Betty. And yet she had so far heard nothing, seen nothing.

"Look through the opening in the curtain toward the farthest end of the room--there by the big closet door," Betty whispered. "Be perfectly still, for I am quite sure that the figure has passed entirely around the room twice as though it were groping for something. I can't see, I can only hear it, and once I felt sure that a hand touched our bed."

Shadowy, terrifyingly silent, an indistinct outline was discernible along the opposite wall and a hand moving slowly up and down it as if searching for something. Could it be for the door of the closet only a few feet away?

Both girls for the moment were too frightened or too surprised to stir or to call out. The idea of jumping suddenly from the bed and running toward the intruder had occurred to Betty, who was the more widely awake, although she had confessed to herself that she was neither brave nor foolish enough to do it. For the figure was too mysterious, too uncertain, and whether man or woman, boy or girl, she had no conception. Why, it was only the fact of the hand which proved that it was even human!

Then both girls lay rigid once more, with not a muscle moving, scarcely believing that they breathed. For the form was again flitting down the length of the room, possibly toward their bed. The next second and it had passed through Betty's evidently unlatched door and vanished noiselessly into the hall.

Polly was sleeping on the outside of the bed, so it was she who first leaped upon the floor, turning on the electric light until the room was brilliantly illuminated.

"You are not to stir until I can go along with you," Betty protested, following her immediately. And then both girls lost a moment of time in putting on their dressing gowns, for the night was bitterly cold.

"Shall we call somebody first?" Polly inquired, all at once in the lighted room feeling uncertain as to whether the experience through which they had lately passed had been a real one. Nothing in their room was changed in the least since their going to bed. There were Betty's clothes on one chair and her own upon another.

There was the book she had been reading left open upon the desk, and Betty's unfinished letter to Esther. Had they both gone suddenly mad?

But Betty had lighted a candle; so Polly followed until they were able to light the gas in the second story hall.

There was no one about. All the other bedroom doors were safely closed and the Professor was apparently snoring hoarsely.

"Shall we call your mother or wake up anybody?" Polly questioned. But Betty shook her head. She looked pale, and her eyes were uncomfortably mystified. Otherwise she appeared perfectly self-controlled.

"No, let us not call anybody and not mention our alarm until morning. If our visitor was a burglar, he knows that we are aware of his presence and so won't try any more performances tonight. And if it wasn't a burglar, but a ghost, why, there is no use frightening mother to death and we will only get laughed at by the others. It seems queer to me for either a ghost or a burglar to come into a house so filled with people. If you don't mind, Polly, let us just go on back to bed and leave the light burning for our consolation. We had both better try to sleep."

Sleep, however, after their few moments of terror and in the face of the enigma of their unexplained visitor, was impossible. Also the light in the bedroom did not induce slumber, although both girls found it agreeable. Their door leading out into the corridor was now securely latched, notwithstanding that Betty was not in the habit of locking it.

"Betty," Polly asked after a few moments of silence, when the two friends were back again in bed with their arms clasped close about each other, "the closet there at the end of your room--is it one where either you or your mother keep your clothes?"

"No," the other girl repeated thoughtfully. "I had not thought of that. But it only makes things queerer than ever. For the closet is a particularly large one and has always been stored with rubbish. It has an old trunk in it and some pictures and boxes. I don't think there is anything of value, though I don't know exactly what is in the trunk, or the boxes either for that matter. I have often meant to clear the place out, but I have never needed the space and mother pokes around in it sometimes. It is ridiculous to suppose that a burglar would take an interest in old trash, when there are so many other valuable things about. Besides, suppose there should happen to be a few treasures in one of the boxes or the trunk, nobody could know about it when I don't. Oh dear, I wish it were morning!"

Betty sighed deeply, tumbling about restlessly in a fashion that made her a very undesirable bed companion. And yet Polly, who was ordinarily nervous from the slightest movement, made no protest. And she said nothing more for some time, although it was self-evident that she was not growing sleepy. Her rather oddly shaped blue eyes had a far-away, almost uncanny light in them, that somehow added to Betty's discomfort.

"Look here, Polly O'Neill," she protested, giving her arm an affectionate squeeze, "please don't be wishing a ghost upon us. I know you have always believed in Irish fairies and elves and hobgoblins and the like, and used to fuss with poor Mollie and me outrageously because we couldn't or wouldn't see them. But tonight--Oh, well, even Irish ghosts don't come strolling into one's bedroom. They at least have the courtesy to stay in churchyards and in haunted ruins."

"Yes, but isn't this the haunted room of this house, Betty?" Polly inquired in a faintly teasing voice, which yet held a note of serious questioning in it.

And immediately Betty's face grew white and frightened, far more so than at any moment before during their adventure, so that the other girl was instantly regretful of her speech.

"Polly O'Neill," two firm hands next took hold on Polly's thin shoulders, turning her deliberately over in bed so that she was forced to face her questioner, "ever since I can remember there has been some mystery or other connected with this old room. Of course it is not haunted. I suppose sensible people don't believe in ghosts, though I don't see why not believing makes them fail to exist. But the room may have had a tragedy of some kind take place in it, something that both mother and Dick find it painful to mention or recall. I told you that mother would not explain her feeling to me when I insisted upon knowing. However, I don't think my family has the right to keep a secret from me. I am nearly grown now and no longer the kind of girl I used to be. So see here, Polly. Look me directly in the eyes. Oftentimes outsiders hear things first. Have you ever heard of a sorrow or accident, or even something worse, that may have occurred in this house or even in this room when I was too little a girl to understand or remember it? You must tell me the truth."

Polly shook her head, devoutly thankful at the moment for her own lack of information. With Betty's beautiful, honest gray eyes searching her own, with her lips trembling and her cheeks flushed with the fervor of her desire, her friend would have found deceiving her extremely difficult. Yet it was more agreeable to change the subject of their talk, even though it continued upon dangerous grounds.

"No, Betty, I was not thinking of ghosts nor of the fact that you have always been absurdly curious about the mystery of this room. I was thinking of something altogether different--of a thief, in fact--and I was wondering whether you would be angry or hurt or both if I mention something to you?" Polly returned.

Betty kissed her friend's thin cheek, wishing at the same instant that it would grow more rounded, now that Polly was presumably well. "You don't usually mind making me angry, dear," she smiled. "And I don't see why if you have a possible theory of a burglar that I should be hurt. Do you think the figure we saw was a man's or a woman's?"

"I don't know," the other girl replied. "What I have been wondering is just this: Has any one in this house ever come into this room with your mother when she was rummaging in that old closet, to help her move the furniture or lift things about?"

For a moment Betty frowned and then her face flamed crimson.

"You are not fair, Polly. You never have approved of his living here or my being kind to him. And you have said half a dozen times that there was no special point in my being particularly grateful to him, since any one of our friends would have done just what he did, had they been equally near me. But then of course that does not alter the fact. Now just because *he* has been in here to assist mother does not prove anything, does not even make it fair to be suspicious."

Polly shrugged her shoulders. "I knew you would be angry, so I am sorry I spoke. But you see our first meeting in the woods with the young man when your safety box was almost stolen from you was a little unfortunate. But I don't say that I suspect any one, either, and I have no intention of not being fair. However, I do intend to keep on the lookout. Now kiss me good morning, for I am going to turn out the light. The gray dawn seems at last to be breaking and perhaps we may both get a little sleep before breakfast time."

CHAPTER XVIII
UNCERTAINTY

In spite of their own entire conviction the story told the next day by Polly and Betty to the various members of the Ashton household was received with little credulity. Even Mrs. Ashton was inclined to be skeptical after finding that nothing in the big house had been stolen or even disarranged. There was no window that had been pried open and no door left unlocked. Then why, even if the robber had entered the house by some mysterious process of his own, had he gone away again empty-handed? There were many pieces of valuable silver in the lower part of the establishment, pictures, even single ornaments that could be sold for fair sums of money. Therefore why climb to the second story and enter the girls' room first?

Although Betty and Polly were too deeply offended by the suggestion to allow it to be freely discussed, Miss McMurtry's idea that they had had a kind of sympathetic nightmare, or at least a mutual hallucination, was the most commonly accepted theory. It was an extremely annoying point of view to both the girls, of course, but as they had nothing to disprove it, they were obliged after several futile arguments to let the matter rest. Naturally their Camp Fire friends were delightfully thrilled by the anecdote, but as it was always received either with open or carefully concealed disbelief, after a few days neither Polly nor Betty cared to speak of it except to each other.

There was one person, however, who, whether or not he believed the truth of their story, at least accepted it with extreme seriousness. And it was to him that Polly O'Neill made a determined effort to be the first narrator of their experience.

Anthony Graham was in the habit of getting up earlier than any one else in the Ashton house and had of course disappeared hours before either of the girls awakened the morning after their nearly sleepless night. However, he was accustomed to returning to his small room in the third story at about half-past five o'clock every afternoon, when his work for the day was over, in order to change his clothes for the evening. So at about this time Polly found it convenient to be in the hallway leading to his room and to be there alone.

As he walked toward her unconscious of her presence, in spite of her prejudice against him she could not fail to see how much the young man had improved. He was hardly recognizable as the boy with whom they had had the encounter in the woods a little more than a year before. He was shabby enough and as lean as a young animal that has had too much exercise and too little food. His face was serious, almost sad; nevertheless Polly had no intention of not pursuing her investigation.

She had seated herself on a narrow window ledge and was presumably peering out at the trees in the garden.

As he caught sight of her the young man started with a perfectly natural surprise. For although Polly had been in the same house with him now for a number of weeks, they had not seen each other more than half a dozen times and had only talked together once when Betty had made a point of introducing them as though they had never met before.

Perhaps some recollection of their original coming together was in Anthony's memory, for he blushed a kind of dull brick red, when Polly, turning deliberately from her window seat, said: "Mr. Graham, I wonder if you would mind giving me a minute of your time. There is something I wish to tell you."

"Certainly," he answered and then stood fingering his hat in the same awkward fashion that he had employed in his Thanksgiving visit to Betty, yet regarding the girl herself with a totally different sensation.

For instinctively Anthony Graham recognized that Polly O'Neill was or might become his enemy. Not that she would do him any wrong, but that if ever he was able to set out to accomplish the desire of his heart, the weight of her influence and feeling would be against him. And he did not underestimate the compelling power of a nature like Polly's. She was wayward, high tempered, sometimes appearing unreliable and almost unloving. Yet this last fact was never true of her. It was only that her personality was of the kind that can want but one thing at a time with all the passion and force of which it is capable. And pursuing this desire, she might seem to forget her other impulses. Polly, however, never did put aside her few really vital affections. She and Betty Ashton might quarrel, might continue to disagree as they had so often done in the past; yet Betty's welfare and happiness would always be of intense concern to her friend. More because of the quality of her imagination than from any single witnessed fact, Polly had lately suspected that Anthony might learn to care more for her friend than would be comfortable for anybody concerned in the affair. And undoubtedly the young man had once been a thief if intention counted. Therefore he might be a thief again, and in any case probably needed to be forewarned of a number of things.

"There was a burglar in our room last night," Polly began, wasting no time in preliminaries, but keeping her blue eyes fixed so directly upon Anthony's that they were like blue flames.

Even before he could reply the young man wondered how there could be people who thought this girl beautiful or even pretty. It was true that at times her eyes were strangely magnetic, that her hair was always black with that peculiar almost dead luster, and her lips like two fine scarlet lines. Yet she was always too thin, her chin too pointed and her cheekbones too high to touch any of his ideals of beauty.

"I--I am sorry. That is--what *do you mean*?" the young fellow stammered stupidly. And all at once the scowl gathered upon his face that Betty Ashton had once misunderstood. It was a black, ugly look, and in this case certainly was inspired by the impression that because of his former misdeed, Polly might now be suspecting him of another.

And she left him no room for doubt.

"Oh, I am not exactly accusing you," she remarked coolly, "for I presume that would hardly be fair. But I am not going to pretend that I feel as much confidence in you as I do in the people against whom I know nothing. I can't. Perhaps I may some day when you have made good, but it is a little too soon to expect it of me, as I am not an idealist like some girls. So last night, though we did not have any reason to suspect that the person who entered our room and then stole out again without our ever really seeing him or her had anything to do with you, I must confess I did think of you. Because, though it is just as well not to talk about it, there is no question but that the intruder was already living in this house. No one came in from the outside. So you see it is like this: I don't begin to say that it was you, but I am going to be on the watch and it is just as fair to warn you openly as to suspect you in secret. Then there is another thing. Personally I don't believe we had a ghostly visitant, as Betty is inclined to think because of the mystery of that particular room. So suppose we take it for granted that you had nothing to do with our experience, then will you help Betty and me to find out who or what it was? We do not want to create too much disturbance over it."

Just how many varying emotions had passed through Anthony Graham's mind during Polly's amazing speech, it would be difficult to express. He was bitterly angry of course, deeply wounded and resentful, and yet he could not but have a certain respect for the girl's outspokenness, for her kind of brutal courage. Certainly he was given notice not to repeat his offense, if offense he had committed. And as proof of his own innocence it might be as wise for him to discover the real offender.

Anthony kept a hold on himself by a fine effort of self-control. The truth was that he and Polly O'Neill were not altogether unlike in disposition, and he had a temper and a will to match with hers. Notwithstanding, he appreciated that this was not the occasion for revealing weakness.

Therefore he merely bowed with such quiet courtesy that Polly was secretly astonished.

"You are unfair in suspecting me of having violated Mrs. Ashton's confidence simply because I once tried to commit a theft. Though of course I know that most people would feel just as you do. Does Betty--does Miss Ashton----" he inquired.

Polly frowned. "No," she responded curtly.

"Then will you tell her, please, that you have confided what has happened to me and that I will do my best to ferret out the mystery."

And Anthony walked past and into his own room, closing the door noiselessly behind him.

With a shrug of her thin shoulders Polly stood for another moment regarding the shut door. "I am sorry to say it, but he has behaved a great deal better than I expected," she thought to herself with a smile at her own expense.

CHAPTER XIX
AN UNSPOKEN POSSIBILITY

The two friends were walking home from school together about ten days later. They had both stayed until almost dusk engaged in different pursuits.

Betty was doing some extra studying with Miss McMurtry, as she had missed so much time and science was always her weakest point; while Polly had been having an hour's quiet talk with her former elocution teacher, Miss Adams. Probably she was the one person in Woodford, excepting Betty, who sympathized in the least with Polly in her escapade. Or if she did not exactly sympathize with her, she was sorry for the retribution that she had brought upon herself. For Mrs. Wharton had decreed that her daughter was not to leave Woodford again and was not even to be permitted to study anything in the village with the view of its being useful to her later in a stage career. The subject was to be entirely tabooed until Polly reached twenty-one, when if she were of the same mind, she might choose her own future. Of course to an impatient nature three years and a few months over seemed like an eternity, and except for Betty's sympathy and her frequent talks with Miss Adams and the latter's accounts of her great cousin, Margaret Adams, Polly believed existence would have been unendurable.

She was in such a state of excitement now over something which Miss Adams had been recently telling her, that at first she hardly heard what Betty was trying to say.

"I have her permission to tell you, Polly dear, because she wishes to have your advice, as you have more imagination about getting out of difficulties than the rest of us; but you have to promise first never to mention it to anybody, not to a single other member of the Camp Fire Club or to Rose or even Donna."

Polly laughed, putting her arm lightly across Betty Ashton's shoulder.

"What are you talking about, child?" she demanded. "I don't particularly like that suggestion of my talent for getting out of scrapes; but if the scrape has anything to do with Betty Ashton, then all my talent is at her disposal, of course."

"But it has nothing to do with me, at least not in the way you mean," the other girl replied, too much in earnest to be amused even for the moment. "It has to do with a girl whom you have never liked very much and she has never liked you. But she has been my friend and I do care for her. And moreover she is a member of our Sunrise Hill Camp Fire Club and we promised to live up to Sylvia's motion."

"Edith Norton?" Polly queried. "She must be in trouble if she is willing to confide in me."

But Betty's expression suddenly silenced her. Always Betty Ashton had been the most popular among her special group of Camp Fire girls. At first chiefly for her beauty, her wealth, the prominent position of her family and for her own generosity and charm. More recently, however, since the girl had met her own disasters so courageously, a new element had come into her influence and the affection she inspired. It was a quality that Polly with all her cleverness would never create, one of steadfastness under fire. Perhaps it was one of the last characteristics that one might have looked for in the early days of the Princess. And yet it will always be found in truly aristocratic natures. When life is flowing smoothly, when the days go by with no special demands made upon them, these persons may have many little weaknesses. Yet when the special occasion arises theirs is the faithfulness and fortitude. So while Betty had neither the sound judgment of Sylvia Wharton nor the brilliant fancy of Polly, it was to her that the other girls usually made their first appeal in any dilemma or distress.

At this moment if they had not been together on the street Polly would have liked to embrace her. The cold air had brought Betty's color back; she still wore the little lace cap under her old fur hat, but the edging made a lovely frame for her face, and her hair was already growing so that the curls showed underneath, like a baby's.

"Yes, it is Edith," Betty answered seriously. "And she is in a difficulty that you could never have imagined of one of our Camp Fire girls. You know she has been going a good deal with that man whom none of us like until she thinks she is really in love with him. And it seems that Edith believes that he does not care a great deal about her. So she, poor thing, has been trying her best to make him care. She has bought herself a lot of clothes that she cannot afford, for you know she gets such a small salary at the shop where she works."

"Is that all?" Polly demanded. "It is awfully foolish of her, of course, to be so extravagant, but it isn't such a dreadful crime. And as I suppose she has charged what she got, she can just save up and pay back her bills by degrees."

Betty shook her head. "Don't be a goose, dear. Edith can't charge things in Woodford. She hasn't any credit in the shops like your mother and mine have. She is only a poor girl working for her own support, with her family not living here and with no position when they were. No, you see she borrowed the money from the woman she was working for without telling her. She meant to pay it back of course, only, only----"

"You mean she stole it from her?" Polly exclaimed in a hushed tone. This was a good deal worse than anything which she had anticipated. She had always considered Edith Norton foolish and vain; but then surely the Camp Fire had helped her, had given her the ideals and the training that she had never learned at home. Betty was crying so bitterly and so openly that Polly felt she must comfort her friend first before criticising or attempting to suggest a solution to the other girl's problem.

"But, dear, if you wish Edith's trouble kept a secret, you must not weep over her, just as you get home," she protested. "Don't you know that everybody in the house will be demanding to know what the matter is at once, and the Professor can hardly be kept from weeping with you? I can't think of anything to suggest to Edith except that she confess what she has done and ask Madame to let her return the money by working for it."

"I told her that, but she did not believe that she would be forgiven," Betty explained. "Oh, if I only had just a little of the money I used to throw away! I don't mind being poor so much myself, Polly; it is when I so want to do for other people."

"You don't have to tell me that, Princess," her friend replied quietly. "But, dear, this time I am glad you have not the money. Because you know it would not be right for you just to give Edith the money and have her give it back without any one's knowing. At least, I don't quite think so. And yet I am awfully sorry that

Edith and I should both in our different ways have broken our Camp Fire law. And I will do anything I can think of to help her. Do you know, dear, how long she has been in this difficulty?

"Oh, I think about two weeks," Betty answered. "But she only confided in me yesterday. It seems that she has tried several ways of getting the money and has attempted to borrow it. She thought maybe I could lend it to her, and I may be able to later on, only I would have to tell mother some reason why I needed twenty-five dollars all of a sudden from our small supply."

"No, you must not. Maybe I may be able to help. Or we may persuade Edith to confess. I believe she will when she thinks more about our old Camp Fire teachings. Anyhow, as we are at home now, let us wait and talk it all over again tonight after we get to bed. It is then, of course, that I do my most brilliant thinking."

So with this in mind, obliterating all other thoughts at their hour of retiring, for the first evening since their fright ten days before, neither Polly nor Betty remembered the locking of their outside door upon getting into bed.

And this time it was Polly O'Neill who was aroused first a short while after midnight by the slow turning of their doorknob and then the sense of an almost noiseless figure entering their bedroom.

Immediately she awoke Betty by suddenly calling her name aloud, and at the same instant sprang out of bed, again touching the electric button and flooding the room with revealing light.

CHAPTER XX
THE BEGINNING OF LIGHT

Why, why!" exclaimed Polly in surprise and consternation, standing perfectly still with her hand upraised toward the light, too puzzled to let it drop down at her side.

But with a little, warning cry Betty had called to her and almost at the same moment was across the room, with her arms about a tall, slight figure.

"Mother, mother," she whispered quietly, "wake up. You have gotten up out of your bed and wandered into Polly's and my room. And you have frightened us nearly to death! Dear me, you have not walked in your sleep for years, have you?"

At Betty's first words following the stream of light, Mrs. Ashton had opened her eyes with returning consciousness until now she appeared almost entirely wide awake. And an expression both of fear and annoyance crossed her face.

"You poor children, so I am your ghost and your burglar," she declared, "and I believed it was you who were having nightmares! I am awfully sorry. Betty knows I used to have this unfortunate habit of strolling about the house in my sleep long ago. But I am quite sure that I have not done it for several years now. The truth is I have not yet gotten over the nervous shock of Betty's being brought home to me and my not knowing how seriously she was injured for such a time; it seemed an eternity."

Betty had thrown a shawl over her mother's shoulders, as she was clad only in her night-dress, and she and Polly slipped into their dressing gowns.

"Wasn't it odd, though, mother, your coming in here both times? I wonder if you had me on your mind and wanted to see how I was. But you did not seem to. You kept groping your way toward that old closet as though you wished to rummage about in it. But do come and let me take you back to bed now, and I will stay with you so you will behave yourself and give Polly a chance to rest."

For quite five minutes after the two had gone, Polly lay awake. There were really so many things to consider, because, of course, when one has too active an imagination it is apt to lead one into trouble. First, she must apologize to Anthony Graham for her totally unfounded suspicion of him. And then, thank Heaven, she had not breathed the suggestion aloud! Yet just for a moment she had wondered if Edith Norton could have--but it was not true and of course never could have been.

Then a third idea. What could be hidden away in that old closet of so great value or interest that Mrs. Ashton turned toward it in her sleeping hours, when her subconscious mind must be directing her footsteps?

No wonder that Betty was puzzled and annoyed over the secrets of the old room. Naturally as a visitor in the Ashton home it would be exceedingly bad manners, if nothing worse, for her to try to find out anything that her hostess wished to keep concealed. Yet just as Polly lost her train of thought she remembered wishing that Betty might make the discovery for herself, since most certainly then she would confide in her.

The next day being Friday, Polly went to her own home to spend the weekend. And quite by accident she and Mollie came in together for a few moments on Sunday afternoon and went directly to Betty's room without letting her know of their approach.

As they knocked and had no answer, Polly, feeling entirely at home, pushed the door open.

"Betty, child, don't you want to see us?" she demanded. "I know I promised to give you a rest until Monday, but Mollie and I could not bear to spend a whole Sunday afternoon without you."

And at this, Betty Ashton appeared from the darkness of the big closet at the farthest end of her bedroom. She wore a lavender cashmere frock with a broad velvet belt and a lace cap with lavender ribbons. But the cap was much awry, so that her hair was tumbled carelessly over her forehead, even showing the slight scar underneath, which usually she was so careful to hide, and her cheeks were a good deal flushed. There was no doubt that she was greatly interested or excited over something.

"Mollie and Polly, I am glad," she avowed. "I was just needing some one to talk to and to ask questions of most dreadfully. Mother has gone out driving this afternoon, and as I was alone it occurred to me it might be fun to rummage about in this old closet and see whether it really concealed any treasures. After our belief that a burglar was trying to enter it, I thought it might be just as well for me to find out what it contained."

"Does your mother know?" Polly inquired, and could hardly have explained to herself just why she asked the question.

"No. I did not think of investigating it before she left. But of course she won't care. Why should she? The boxes have nothing in them but old books and rubbish. But this trunk--I can't quite understand about some of the things I have found in it. Maybe you can help me guess."

And before either of the other girls knew what she intended doing, Betty was dragging the shaky trunk out of the closet into the greater brightness of the room, Mollie rushing to her assistance as soon as possible. Yet for some reason unknown to herself, Polly hesitated. She did not even move forward when Betty and Mollie dropped down on their knees before it, although she did observe that the trunk was locked, but that the hinges at the back had rusted and fallen off, so that Betty had gotten into it in that way.

Evidently the things at the top had already been taken out inside the closet, for Betty was now reaching down toward the bottom and bringing out what looked like a trousseau of baby clothes--her own or Dick's, they could not yet tell which.

The little dresses were yellow and fragile with age; the long blue coat had faded; most of the little shoes and flannels had been worn.

"I wish you would not look through those things until your mother gets back, Betty," Polly said rather irritably.

But both her sister and friend glanced up at her in surprise.

"What is the possible harm? Mother couldn't mind. There is certainly no reason why I should not look at my own clothes or at Dick's. It's queer I never happen to have seen them before."

"Did your mother never have any other children, Betty?" Mollie inquired, and the other girl shook her head.

Polly had come over now and was standing near them by the edge of the trunk and looking down inside it.

Of course what Betty was doing must seem to her perfectly right or else she would never have thought of doing it; yet Polly could not help feeling a certain distaste for the whole proceeding. Old possessions were always kind of uncanny and uncomfortable to her temperament; they held too poignant a suggestion of death, of the passing of time and of almost forgotten memories.

Betty and Mollie had a differently romantic point of view. And to both of them, being essentially feminine, the delicate, exquisite baby apparel made a strongly sentimental appeal.

Suddenly, with a little cry of surprise and amusement, Betty picked up a small frock which must have been made for a child of about a year old, that was curiously different from the others. While they had been of sheer lawns and expensive laces, this was a perfectly straight-up-and-down garment of coarse check gingham of the cheapest kind and attached to it were a pair of rough little shoes.

"I wonder how in the world these ever got in here or why mother has preserved them so carefully. She has a perfect horror of cheap things," Betty began in a half-puzzled and half-humorous fashion, holding the poor little baby dress up to the light and giving it a shake.

Stooping, Mollie picked up something that must have fallen from one of the shoes. It was an old tintype picture of a comparatively young man with a baby in his arms and a little girl pressing close up against his knee.

Mollie was looking at it with a slightly bewildered expression when Polly came up and glanced over her shoulder. And instantly Polly's face grew white; however, it was a trick of hers when anything surprised or annoyed her. And at the moment she had a strong impulse to take the picture from Mollie's hands and tear it into a hundred pieces before Betty Ashton should have a chance to see it.

Notwithstanding, Betty had already joined them and was apparently as much perplexed as Mollie. She took the photograph nearer to the window.

"I declare this looks like Esther when she was a little girl and Professor Crippen. I believe he did tell me there was another child that somebody had adopted and who did not know he was her father. I suppose Esther must have asked mother to take care of these things for her. It is queer that she never thought of speaking of them to me. I must write her I have seen them, for I should not wish her to feel

I had been prying," Betty finished, going back to the trunk and putting the little things carefully away.

The weight that had gathered pressingly in the neighborhood of Polly's heart in the past thirty seconds now lifted.

"Yes, and do close up that tiresome trunk at once Betty Ashton, or I am going home," Polly scolded. "It bores me dreadfully to have you and Mollie poking in there when we might be talking."

But Betty paid no heed to her, for she had found another photograph of a different character. It was a picture of another baby, a beautiful miniature so delicately tinted that the colors were almost like life. And the child's face was very like Mrs. Ashton's, the same flaxen hair and light blue eyes. And it bore no possible resemblance either to Richard Ashton or to Betty. However, there was no reason to consider its being either one of them, for it was plainly marked on the back, "Phyllis Ashton," and then had the date of the birth.

Betty offered no comment and expressed no wonder, although she let both her friends look at the picture, still holding it in her own hands.

"But I thought you said your mother had only two children, you and Dick," Mollie declared, and Polly would have liked to shake her.

"Yes, I did think so until now," the third girl replied. And placing her picture back in the trunk, she closed the lid, still leaving the trunk in the center of the room, in spite of the fact that both her friends insisted on helping her with it into the closet.

Then Betty began making tea on her alcohol lamp and talking of other things; only Polly could see that her mind was not in the least upon what she was saying, but that she was thinking of something else every possible second.

Whether to go or to stay with her friend was Polly's present indecision. However, she and Molly remained until Mrs. Ashton had returned from her drive and Betty went into her mother's room to assist in taking off her wraps.

CHAPTER XXI
BETTY FINDS OUT

It was Monday afternoon and the March weather held an alluring suggestion of spring.

Running along the street with her red coat scarcely fastened and her hat at a totally wrong angle upon her head, Polly O'Neill showed no concern for exterior conditions.

Finding the Ashton front door unlocked she entered without stopping to ring the bell, and made straight, not for Betty's, but for Mrs. Ashton's bedroom. She found her lying upon the bed, though at her visitor's entrance she sat up, appearing quite ill.

"O Mrs. Ashton, why didn't Betty come to school today? Where is she? Has anything happened? I was dreadfully worried when I found she was not at any of her classes, and then when I asked Miss McMurtry whether anything was the matter, she was so queer and mysterious. And when I said I was going to leave school and come here at once, she said that I had better not, that Betty had specially asked to be alone and that even you had not seen her this morning. Donna behaved just as though she knew something about my beloved Betty that I don't. And it is not fair. I am sure Betty would wish me to know. Where is she?"

"Sit down, Polly," Mrs. Ashton returned, getting up from the bed and taking a seat opposite. "I don't know where Betty is just now and I am very uneasy and very unhappy about her. The poor child has had so many things happen in the past year, after being spoiled in every possible way up till then. She was in her own room most of the morning, but about two hours ago sent word to me that she was going out and that I was not to be alarmed if she did not return for some little time. I might as well tell you our secret, dear. I suppose there is no way now to keep people from knowing it eventually and perhaps we have been unkind and unwise in concealing it from Betty so long. I wonder if you have ever dreamed that Betty is Esther Crippen's sister?"

Polly gasped. No, she had not dreamed it. If the suspicion had ever entered her mind, she had put it from her as a self-evident absurdity. Her beautiful, exquisite Princess and Esther and Herr Crippen! It was an impossible association of ideas and of people.

"But it can't be true, Mrs. Ashton," she argued almost angrily, feeling that the room was whirling about and that she was almost ill from the surprise and shock. And if this was her sensation, what could Betty's have been! "Think how lovely Betty is and how utterly unlike either of them. Besides, why have we never known and how did you happen to do it?" Polly dropped her face in her two hands. She so very seldom cried that the effort always hurt her.

"It is a tragic story, dear, and one we have never liked to talk about for all our sakes," Mrs. Ashton replied, showing more self-control than Polly had ever seen her display before.

"Very many years ago I had a baby named Phyllis. Betty tells me that you too saw her picture in the old trunk. Well, Dick was a little boy of about seven, and by some dreadful accident found a loaded pistol in his father's desk and came running into the big back room with it, which in those days was the baby's nursery. You can imagine what happened without my telling you. Dick was a child, and yet the horror of it has altered his entire nature and life. He has always been serious and over-conscientious, always anxious to devote his life to the service of other people as a reparation for a tragedy which was never in the least his fault. It was therefore as much for Dick's sake as for mine that Mr. Ashton persuaded us to adopt a baby in Phyllis' place. So we drove out to the asylum together one day, with our minds not made up and there--there we found our adored Betty. Herr Crippen had just left his two children to be cared for, and Betty was only a baby. But she was the most exquisite little thing you can imagine, the same lovely auburn hair and big serious gray eyes. Dick adored her from the moment that she put her arms about his neck and would not let go when the time came for us to return home. We have always loved her since, Polly, as well as if she had been our own baby--better I almost think. You know what she is, so there is little use for me to say it--'Our Princess', dear. I have always loved your name and the other girls' for her."

"But Herr Crippen and Esther--they are so plain, and except for their gifts, why, compared to Betty they seem so--so ordinary," Polly protested.

"But you must remember that there was a mother, too, and that Herr Crippen has said she was an American and very lovely. I believe her family would have nothing more to do with her because she married a German musician. And then, you see, child, Betty has had many advantages that Esther has not had. It was because Dick and I began slowly to realize that perhaps we had been cruel to Esther in depriving her of her little sister that we finally asked her to come here and live as a kind of companion to Betty. It was a long-delayed kindness and yet Esther has very nobly repaid us; for it seems that when Herr Crippen returned and claimed Esther as his daughter, Esther learned then of Betty's relation to them and it was she who insisted that her father make no sign, realizing how entirely Betty's devotion was given to Dick and Mr. Ashton and to me, even to this old home, which has been her pride for so long."

"Poor, poor little Princess! It will almost break her heart," Polly murmured.

But although Mrs. Ashton wiped a few tears from her eyes, she shook her head.

"Some day you will find out that hearts are harder to break than you now believe. I would almost have given my life to have spared Betty this knowledge, and yet some day she must realize that we love her as we have always done and that love is the only thing that greatly counts, after all. There is no reason why Betty should feel any shame in her relation to Herr Crippen; he has been unfortunate, but there is nothing else against him. And Esther is a remarkable girl."

"Yes, I know. But what made Betty suspect? How did she find all this out?" Polly queried.

"Betty told me of her discoveries in the old trunk and asked me a number of questions. I was confused; I am not in the least sure how I answered them. Anyhow, she became suspicious and went to Herr Crippen and then to Miss McMurtry, who, it seems, was in Esther's and her father's confidence. They gave the child no satisfaction, but only made her the more uneasy and distressed, until finally Betty remembered the sealed envelope which Mr. Ashton had always made her keep in her box of valuable papers. Possibly she has told you that the envelope was only to be opened when she should come to some crisis in her life and need advice or information. Betty opened the envelope and it contained the papers proving her legal adoption by us and her right in the equal division of whatever property either Mr. Ashton or I might have. Now, Polly, that is all," Mrs. Ashton concluded. "But I feel that if Betty does not soon come to me and put her arms about me and call me 'mother' as she always has, that I shan't be able to bear things either. Won't you find her and bring her here to me?"

And Polly, glad to be away to battle with her own emotions, kissed her older friend and vanished. But Betty was not in her room, and as there seemed to be no clue to work upon, it was difficult to decide just where she should begin the search.

CHAPTER XXII
SUNRISE CABIN

Betty was not with any one of their acquaintances, for Polly telephoned everybody they knew before leaving the Ashton house.

Then a possibility suddenly dawning upon her, she hurried forth, feeling that anything was better than remaining longer indoors.

All of the Sunrise Hill Camp Fire girls were in the habit of taking frequent walks to their forsaken log cabin. And as Betty wished to be alone and especially needed the strength and consolation that its happy memories could give her, probably she had gone out there. Under most circumstances Polly would have respected her friend's desire for solitude, but Betty must already have been at the cabin for some time by herself and the dusk would soon come down upon her and she would be hurt and lonely, with all her familiar world fallen about her feet.

No one else must learn of her pilgrimage, since Betty might forgive her presence and yet could not rally to meet the astonishment and sympathy of any other of her friends. So Polly told several impatient fibs to the persons who insisted upon learning where she intended going, before she was able to get outside of Woodford and into the blessed solitude of the country lanes.

The air was colder by this time and light flurries of snow kept blinding her eyes as she hurried along. However, she had not so forgotten her training in woodcraft as not to recognize signs of Betty's having preceded her along almost the same route; for here and there, where the earth had thawed in the midday warmth, there were impressions of the Princess' shoes. And she even picked up a small crushed handkerchief which had been dropped by the way.

Therefore in spite of her depression over Mrs. Ashton's information, Polly was beginning to get a kind of hold upon herself. For it was her place, if she possibly could manage it, to persuade Betty that, after all, life was not so utterly changed by yesterday's discovery. If Mrs. Ashton and Dick were not her own mother and brother, they themselves knew no difference. And there would be no change in her friends' affections. Then, she had gained Esther as a sister, Esther who was so big in her nature, so unselfish and fine. No wonder she had always seemed to care for Betty with a devotion no one of them could explain. And how hard it must have been loving her as she did to have made no claim upon her.

"Hello, Miss Polly," an unexpected voice cried out, and to Polly's utter vexation she beheld Billy Webster coming toward her from the path that led through his father's woods.

She bowed coldly, hoping that her coldness might be her salvation, since she did not wish to waste time in conversation with him, nor to explain why she was in such a hurry to go on with her walk. But Billy was apparently not influenced by Polly's present attitude, being too accustomed to her moods.

"May I walk along with you?" he inquired politely enough. "I was just out for exercise, with no special place in mind where I wished to go, and I should ever so much rather have you as a companion."

It was on the tip of Polly's tongue to exclaim, "But I would so much rather not have you!" However, she suddenly recalled having promised Mollie to be as polite to Billy as she could and not to bear malice any longer. So she merely shook her head. "I am sorry, but I am in a great hurry," she explained. "For you see I came out with a very special place in mind to which I wish to go immediately."

Billy laughed, rather a big, splendid, open-hearted laugh. Polly was amusing, in no matter what temper she might happen to be.

"But I won't interfere with your destination and I certainly can manage to walk as fast as you can," he announced calmly, keeping close to the girl's side, although her rapid walking had developed almost into a run, and she was nearly out of breath.

Well, if she could not outwalk him and could not manage to get rid of him in any other way, Polly decided that she would at least keep perfectly silent until he had the sense to go away of his own accord. It was still some distance before she could reach the cabin.

However, as Billy was doing a great deal of talking, he appeared not to be aware of her unusual silence.

"Look here, Miss Polly, I have been thinking of something for a long time--several months, in fact," he declared. "And I have about come to the conclusion that maybe I was pretty domineering in the way in which I behaved to you in New York. Of course I still consider that acting business a dreadful thing for you to have done which might have brought consequences that you could not imagine. But I ought to have tried to persuade you to stop or to write your mother, and not to have bullied you. I want you to believe, though, that it was because I like you so much that I went all to pieces over the idea of anything happening to you--your getting ill or somebody being rude to you. Great Scott! but I am glad that you have given up that foolish idea of going upon the stage and have settled down quietly in Woodford!"

Polly turned a pair of astonished blue eyes upon her companion, who happened at the moment to be gazing up toward the sky where the snow clouds were growing heavier.

"You are very kind to be interested in my welfare, I am sure," she replied, trying her best not to let sarcastic tones creep into her voice. "And of course I realized that your friendship for Mollie and mother made you feel that you had the right to express your opinion very frankly to me. But you are mistaken if you believe that I have given up my foolish notion of going upon the stage. Of course I appreciate now that I was wrong in betraying mother's trust and in trying that experiment in acting without her consent. So I have accepted my punishment and made my bargain. But just the same, when I am twenty-one, I mean to try again with all my strength and power and to keep on trying until I ultimately succeed."

Billy Webster closed his lips with a look of peculiar obstinacy.

"Three years is a long time," he answered, "and you might as well know that though I am fond of Mollie and always will be, it is you I really care about. Oh yes, I realize that there are hours when I almost hate you, but that is because you dislike me and because I can't get you to do what I wish. Still, you might as well understand that I intend doing everything in my power for the next three years to make you stay in Woodford when the time is up and to make you stay because you love me."

And then before Polly was able to get her breath or to stamp her foot or in any possible way to relieve her feelings, the young man had marched away through an opening at one side of the path, without even stopping once to glance back at her.

It was out of the question then for Polly to decide whether she was the more angry, astonished or amused. Of course it was absurd for Billy Webster to conceive of having any emotion for her except one of disapproval. He was simply so obstinate and so sure of himself that he wanted to make her like him, because he knew that she almost hated him. And if it had not been for Mollie, she would have suffered no "almost" in her dislike.

Really the confusion and protest that the young man's words had awakened in her mind, coming on top of the disclosure about Betty, made Polly feel as if she had suddenly taken leave of her senses. And as it is a rather good scheme when one is unable to think clearly, to give up thinking at all for the time being, the girl started running in the direction of the cabin, so fast that she had opportunity for no other impulse or impression except forcing herself to keep up the desired speed.

By a camp fire, which Betty had built for herself, Polly discovered her friend sitting on a stool with her elbow in her lap and her head resting on her hand. She did not seem astonished or annoyed by her friend's entrance. When Polly came forward and kissed her she merely said, "I am glad you know, Polly. I hope you did not have a very cold walk. It was not snowing when I came out." Then she began piling more logs on her fire.

Later the two girls had an intimate talk.

"It is odd, Polly, but I don't feel as wretched as I should have expected I would," Betty explained, speaking as much to herself as to her companion. "I think perhaps it is intended for me to have my illusions shattered earlier in life than other people have them--I think possibly because I have been vainer and more foolish. At first I presume I used to have a kind of unconscious satisfaction in our having more money than other people and in being able to do almost anything for my friends that I wished. Then when the money went away I thought, well, perhaps money does not make so much difference if one has an old family and a name of which one may be proud. But in these last few hours, sitting here by myself I have begun to appreciate more fully what our Camp Fire organization is trying so hard to teach us. It is that all we girls are alike in the essential things, only that some of us have been given better opportunities and more friends. There is only one thing that really counts, I suppose, and that is not so much what other people do for us, as what we are able to do for ourselves, what kind of women we are able to grow into. So you see that though I believe I was struggling to save the old Ashton house because all my distinguished ancestors had been living there for generation after generation and I wanted to have babies of my own to inherit it some day, now I am even happier because perhaps I have saved it for Dick and mother by my plan and maybe it will repay them a little for all they have done for me."

"I don't think the debt is on your side, dear," Polly returned loyally.

But already Betty had risen from her stool and was looking around for her cloak and cap.

"Let us hurry home now; we shall have a glorious walk!" she exclaimed. "I have been away from mother long enough and I do want to write to Esther. She has got to come to see me for a few days, or else I am going to her. Don't worry; I shall not forget the seven points of our Camp Fire star."

CHAPTER XXIII
FAREWELLS

One morning in May two months later two girls were in the much-discussed back bedroom overlooking the Ashton garden. It was very much the same kind of cheerless day outdoors that it had been when they had first met each other after a lapse of many years. And then of course neither one knew of the closeness of the tie between them. However, at the present moment they were busily engaged in packing two steamer trunks that were standing open before them.

"I never shall get all this stuff in if you don't come and help me, Esther," Betty protested in the spoiled fashion of an earlier time. And since Esther never would cease to believe that the whole world should be grateful to Betty for the honor of her presence in it, it is doubtful whether her methods of spoiling "The Princess" ever would be entirely given up.

"Sit down, dear, or else run and see Polly and Mollie and Mrs. Wharton for a few moments. You are tired and I can finish putting the things in for you without any trouble. Poor Polly is kind of pathetic these days, I think; she is so desperate over our going away and leaving her behind, and then, though she tries her best not to show it, she is jealous of our being so much together. I am sorry for her, because it is pretty much the same way that I used to feel toward her. And of course I have tried to show her that no one can take her place with you; but she is so low-spirited and so unlike herself that there is no convincing her of anything agreeable."

Betty had sunk into a low chair and was rocking thoughtfully back and forward knitting her brows.

"Mother and I both consider that Mrs. Wharton is making a mistake in not allowing Polly to leave Woodford for three years; for she will probably grow so tired of it by that time that she will never want to come home again--that is, if she goes on the stage. When it was decided that we were to go abroad mother suggested to Mrs. Wharton that she let Polly come over and join us later. She thought it would be very much more apt to distract her attention than if she stayed on here with nothing else to dream about."

"And what did Mrs. Wharton answer?" Esther queried, turning from her own trunk and beginning to straighten out the confusion in her sister's.

"Oh, she wouldn't hear of it," Betty returned. "So sometimes I feel pretty self-ish at being so happy over our sailing. But just think, we are going straight to Germany and dear old Dick! It seems a hundred years since he went away. How strangely things have turned out! Here are Miss McMurtry and my new father get-ting married, when I have been predicting that they would, with no one believing me, ever since that evening at the cabin. So they will be able to look after the house and let the people stay on in it just as if mother and I were here, and send us a check for the rent each month so that we will have enough to live upon. But better than anything, Esther dear, is the wonderful chance you will have for your music. You are going to study under one of the greatest teachers in the world and not because of what your own family believe about your talent, but because of what your teacher in New York wrote the Professor." It was not often that Betty was able to speak of Herr Crippen as father; Mr. Ashton had been her father too long, and she had cared for him too much to be willing to give the title to any one else. So "the Professor" and "Donna" were the names she ordinarily bestowed upon her new parents.

"You must not expect too much of my singing, Betty," Esther replied in her same shy, nervous fashion. "And, for goodness sake! don't write your brother Dick that my voice has improved, or he will be disappointed."

Betty laughed teasingly. "Oh, I have told him already that you were greater than Melba and Farrar rolled into one. But never mind, Esther, he will soon find out the real truth for himself. Isn't it too splendid how happy mother is over our plans! She has not been so like herself since father's death. And somehow instead of acting as if she had given me up to the Professor as a daughter, she behaves far more as if he had just presented her with you as well. I believe she feels it helps to make up to you, Esther, for the years of loneliness--her being able now to chaperon you, when you so much need to have your big chance."

Esther was kneeling on the floor; but she turned her light blue eyes appealingly upon her sister and her lips quivered, revealing her one beautiful feature in the mobility of the lines of her mouth and in the whiteness of her teeth.

"You must not expect too much of me, little sister, will you?" she pleaded. "You know I have only consented to father's making this big sacrifice for me so that we may all be abroad together, and you and Mrs. Ashton have the rest and change you so much need. And then, of course, I may be able to learn to sing well enough some day to earn the money to buy you a Paris frock and hat," she ended with an attempt at lightness.

However, Betty was not deceived, and getting up from her rocking chair, she deliberately pushed Esther aside.

"For goodness sake! let me finish packing my own trunk, Esther Crippen," she commanded. "Here I have been carefully trying to cultivate an angelic character ever since I became a Camp Fire girl, and in a few weeks of your spoiling you do away with the labor of years."

Betty therefore was not looking up when some one tiptoed quietly into the room, and, before she became conscious of her presence, dropped a bunch of May blossoms under her eyes.

"There are two automobiles waiting before your door at the present moment, children," Polly announced. "And John Everett suggested that I tell you to get into your coats and hats at once. He came home for the day; I've an idea he may have desired to say farewell to 'My Lady Betty,' but I was given no such information. What I was told to say was that he and Meg were giving an automobile ride in your honor and that we were to end up by having our lunch at the cabin. They have asked all the Camp Fire Club and some of John's friends, Billy Webster," and Polly's face expressed her chagrin. "John has even invited Anthony Graham, and the poor fellow has fixed himself up until he is positively shining with cleanliness, though I am afraid he will be cold in that shabby overcoat of his."

While Polly was chattering, she was assisting Betty to slip into her new violet dress which had been made for the steamer crossing and happily was lying ready and spread out upon the bed. And the next instant she had pinned Esther's new blue *crepe de chine* blouse down in the back, hurried them both into their heavy coats and hats, and was ushering them out to their friends, who were impatiently awaiting their coming.

No one of the little party forgot their May day together in the woods and at the Sunrise Hill cabin for a long time to come. And among the many kind things that were said to her in farewell, it was curious that the speech made by Anthony Graham should make the deepest impression upon Betty Ashton's mind.

He had asked her come away from her other friends for a few moments, and they had walked to the edge of the group of pines not far from the foot of Sunrise Hill. It was almost sunset, for no one had thought of going home after the late luncheon was over.

Betty glanced about her rather wistfully. This particular bit of country was dearer to her than any place in the world except her old home and yet she was leaving it for an unknown land, to be away she could not tell how long.

"Miss Ashton," Anthony began, "there will probably be a good many changes in people and things before you come home again. And I am hoping with all my strength that of the greatest changes will have taken place in me. I mean that by that time you need not be ashamed of having befriended me. It is pretty hard sometimes to climb a hill along with other people when you have started so much nearer the bottom than they have. But I feel now that I have made at least a fair start. Judge Maynard told me yesterday that he believed I meant business and that he would teach me all the law he knew and that he would see that I wasn't far behind the fellows at the law schools when the time came for my examinations."

Betty's face glowed with interest and enthusiasm and she gave her two hands to the young man with the same friendliness which she had used in his first call upon her.

"I am so glad, so glad!" she answered. "But please don't speak of my feeling ashamed of you ever again. I know I was rather horrid to you once and that afterwards you saved my life, or what perhaps means more than one's life. Suppose we promise to repay our debts to each other in some entirely new way when we meet after my return." Betty made her idle speech with no special meaning attached to it. And although Anthony agreed in much the same manner, it was possibly fortunate that Betty did not observe his expression as he turned away and walked a few paces ahead of her, gazing up toward the summit of Sunrise Hill. The golden disk of the sun was at this instant resting upon it like the crown of the world. And to

Anthony it seemed none too beautiful or too magnificent a gift to have laid at the feet of a gray-eyed Princess.

Voices were heard calling to them from the cabin, and a short while after good-nights were said and Sunrise Cabin was once more left to solitude and memories.

*   *   *   *   *   *

The next volume of the Camp Fire Girls' Series will be known as "The Camp Fire Girls Across the Seas." Several years will have intervened between it and the previous book and the girls will be introduced under very different influences and circumstances. Just how many of them will have crossed the seas and for what purposes, and how the old Camp Fire influence will still follow them, it is the plan of this story to reveal.

The Codes Of Hammurabi And Moses
W. W. Davies

QTY

The discovery of the Hammurabi Code is one of the greatest achievements of archaeology, and is of paramount interest, not only to the student of the Bible, but also to all those interested in ancient history...

Religion   **ISBN:** *1-59462-338-4*   **Pages:132**
MSRP $12.95

The Theory of Moral Sentiments
Adam Smith

QTY

This work from 1749. contains original theories of conscience amd moral judgment and it is the foundation for systemof morals.

Philosophy **ISBN:** *1-59462-777-0*   **Pages:536**
MSRP $19.95

Jessica's First Prayer
Hesba Stretton

QTY

In a screened and secluded corner of one of the many railway-bridges which span the streets of London there could be seen a few years ago, from five o'clock every morning until half past eight, a tidily set-out coffee-stall, consisting of a trestle and board, upon which stood two large tin cans, with a small fire of charcoal burning under each so as to keep the coffee boiling during the early hours of the morning when the work-people were thronging into the city on their way to their daily toil...

Pages:84

Childrens   **ISBN:** *1-59462-373-2*   *MSRP $9.95*

My Life and Work
Henry Ford

QTY

Henry Ford revolutionized the world with his implementation of mass production for the Model T automobile. Gain valuable business insight into his life and work with his own auto-biography... "We have only started on our development of our country we have not as yet, with all our talk of wonderful progress, done more than scratch the surface. The progress has been wonderful enough but..."

Pages:300

Biographies/   **ISBN:** *1-59462-198-5*   *MSRP $21.95*

The Art of Cross-Examination
Francis Wellman

QTY

I presume it is the experience of every author, after his first book is published upon an important subject, to be almost overwhelmed with a wealth of ideas and illustrations which could readily have been included in his book, and which to his own mind, at least, seem to make a second edition inevitable. Such certainly was the case with me; and when the first edition had reached its sixth impression in five months, I rejoiced to learn that it seemed to my publishers that the book had met with a sufficiently favorable reception to justify a second and considerably enlarged edition. ..

Pages:412

Reference   **ISBN: *1-59462-647-2***   *MSRP $19.95*

On the Duty of Civil Disobedience
Henry David Thoreau

QTY

Thoreau wrote his famous essay, On the Duty of Civil Disobedience, as a protest against an unjust but popular war and the immoral but popular institution of slave-owning. He did more than write—he declined to pay his taxes, and was hauled off to gaol in consequence. Who can say how much this refusal of his hastened the end of the war and of slavery ?

Law   **ISBN: *1-59462-747-9***   **Pages:48**

MSRP $7.45

Dream Psychology Psychoanalysis for Beginners
Sigmund Freud

QTY

Sigmund Freud, born Sigismund Schlomo Freud (May 6, 1856 - September 23, 1939), was a Jewish-Austrian neurologist and psychiatrist who co-founded the psychoanalytic school of psychology. Freud is best known for his theories of the unconscious mind, especially involving the mechanism of repression; his redefinition of sexual desire as mobile and directed towards a wide variety of objects; and his therapeutic techniques, especially his understanding of transference in the therapeutic relationship and the presumed value of dreams as sources of insight into unconscious desires.

Pages:196

Psychology   **ISBN: *1-59462-905-6***   *MSRP $15.45*

The Miracle of Right Thought
Orison Swett Marden

QTY

Believe with all of your heart that you will do what you were made to do. When the mind has once formed the habit of holding cheerful, happy, prosperous pictures, it will not be easy to form the opposite habit. It does not matter how improbable or how far away this realization may see, or how dark the prospects may be, if we visualize them as best we can, as vividly as possible, hold tenaciously to them and vigorously struggle to attain them, they will gradually become actualized, realized in the life. But a desire, a longing without endeavor, a yearning abandoned or held indifferently will vanish without realization.

Pages:360

Self Help   **ISBN: *1-59462-644-8***   *MSRP $25.45*

QTY

The Rosicrucian Cosmo-Conception Mystic Christianity *by Max Heindel*   ISBN: 1-59462-188-8   **$38.95**
The Rosicrucian Cosmo-conception is not dogmatic, neither does it appeal to any other authority than the reason of the student. It is: not controversial, but is: sent forth in the, hope that it may help to clear...   New Age/Religion Pages 646

Abandonment To Divine Providence *by Jean-Pierre de Caussade*   ISBN: 1-59462-228-0   **$25.95**
"The Rev. Jean Pierre de Caussade was one of the most remarkable spiritual writers of the Society of Jesus in France in the 18th Century. His death took place at Toulouse in 1751. His works have gone through many editions and have been republished...   Inspirational/Religion Pages 400

Mental Chemistry *by Charles Haanel*   ISBN: 1-59462-192-6   **$23.95**
Mental Chemistry allows the change of material conditions by combining and appropriately utilizing the power of the mind. Much like applied chemistry creates something new and unique out of careful combinations of chemicals the mastery of mental chemistry...   New Age/Business Pages 354

The Letters of Robert Browning and Elizabeth Barret Barrett 1845-1846 vol II   ISBN: 1-59462-193-4   **$35.95**
by Robert Browning and Elizabeth Barrett   Biographies Pages 596

Gleanings In Genesis (volume I) *by Arthur W. Pink*   ISBN: 1-59462-130-6   **$27.45**
Appropriately has Genesis been termed "the seed plot of the Bible" for in it we have, in germ form, almost all of the great doctrines which are afterwards fully developed in the books of Scripture which follow...   Religion/Inspirational Pages 420

The Master Key *by L. W. de Laurence*   ISBN: 1-59462-001-6   **$30.95**
In no branch of human knowledge has there been a more lively increase of the spirit of research during the past few years than in the study of Psychology, Concentration and Mental Discipline. The requests for authentic lessons in Thought Control, Mental Discipline and...   New Age/Religion Pages 422

The Lesser Key Of Solomon Goetia *by L. W. de Laurence*   ISBN: 1-59462-092-X   **$9.95**
This translation of the first book of the "Lernegton" which is now for the first time made accessible to students of Talismanic Magic was done, after careful collation and edition, from numerous Ancient Manuscripts in Hebrew, Latin, and French...   New Age/Occult Pages 92

Rubaiyat Of Omar Khayyam *by Edward Fitzgerald*   ISBN:1-59462-332-5   **$13.95**
Edward Fitzgerald, whom the world has already learned, in spite of his own efforts to remain within the shadow of anonymity, to look upon as one of the rarest poets of the century, was born at Bredfield, in Suffolk, on the 31st of March, 1809. He was the third son of John Purcell...   Music Pages 172

Ancient Law *by Henry Maine*   ISBN: 1-59462-128-4   **$29.95**
The chief object of the following pages is to indicate some of the earliest ideas of mankind, as they are reflected in Ancient Law, and to point out the relation of those ideas to modern thought.   Religion/History Pages 452

Far-Away Stories *by William J. Locke*   ISBN: 1-59462-129-2   **$19.45**
"Good wine needs no bush, but a collection of mixed vintages does. And this book is just such a collection. Some of the stories I do not want to remain buried for ever in the museum files of dead magazine-numbers an author's not unpardonable vanity..."   Fiction Pages 272

Life of David Crockett *by David Crockett*   ISBN: 1-59462-250-7   **$27.45**
"Colonel David Crockett was one of the most remarkable men of the times in which he lived. Born in humble life, but gifted with a strong will, an indomitable courage, and unremitting perseverance...   Biographies/New Age Pages 424

Lip-Reading *by Edward Nitchie*   ISBN: 1-59462-206-X   **$25.95**
Edward B. Nitchie, founder of the New York School for the Hard of Hearing, now the Nitchie School of Lip-Reading, Inc, wrote "LIP-READING Principles and Practice". The development and perfecting of this meritorious work on lip-reading was an undertaking...   How-to Pages 400

A Handbook of Suggestive Therapeutics, Applied Hypnotism, Psychic Science   ISBN: 1-59462-214-0   **$24.95**
by Henry Munro   Health/New Age/Health/Self-help Pages 376

A Doll's House: and Two Other Plays *by Henrik Ibsen*   ISBN: 1-59462-112-8   **$19.95**
Henrik Ibsen created this classic when in revolutionary 1848 Rome. Introducing some striking concepts in playwriting for the realist genre, this play has been studied the world over.   Fiction/Classics/Plays 308

The Light of Asia *by sir Edwin Arnold*   ISBN: 1-59462-204-3   **$13.95**
In this poetic masterpiece, Edwin Arnold describes the life and teachings of Buddha. The man who was to become known as Buddha to the world was born as Prince Gautama of India but he rejected the worldly riches and abandoned the reigns of power when...   Religion/History/Biographies Pages 170

The Complete Works of Guy de Maupassant *by Guy de Maupassant*   ISBN: 1-59462-157-8   **$16.95**
"For days and days, nights and nights, I had dreamed of that first kiss which was to consecrate our engagement, and I knew not on what spot I should put my lips..."   Fiction/Classics Pages 240

The Art of Cross-Examination *by Francis L. Wellman*   ISBN: 1-59462-309-0   **$26.95**
Written by a renowned trial lawyer, Wellman imparts his experience and uses case studies to explain how to use psychology to extract desired information through questioning.   How-to/Science/Reference Pages 408

Answered or Unanswered? *by Louisa Vaughan*   ISBN: 1-59462-248-5   **$10.95**
Miracles of Faith in China   Religion Pages 112

The Edinburgh Lectures on Mental Science (1909) *by Thomas*   ISBN: 1-59462-008-3   **$11.95**
This book contains the substance of a course of lectures recently given by the writer in the Queen Street Hall, Edinburgh. Its purpose is to indicate the Natural Principles governing the relation between Mental Action and Material Conditions...   New Age/Psychology Pages 148

Ayesha *by H. Rider Haggard*   ISBN: 1-59462-301-5   **$24.95**
Verily and indeed it is the unexpected that happens! Probably if there was one person upon the earth from whom the Editor of this, and of a certain previous history, did not expect to hear again...   Classics Pages 380

Ayala's Angel *by Anthony Trollope*   ISBN: 1-59462-352-X   **$29.95**
The two girls were both pretty, but Lucy who was twenty-one who was to be simple and comparatively unattractive, whereas Ayala was credited, as her Bombwhat romantic name might show, with poetic charm and a taste for romance. Ayala when her father died was nineteen...   Fiction Pages 484

The American Commonwealth *by James Bryce*   ISBN: 1-59462-286-8   **$34.45**
An interpretation of American democratic political theory. It examines political mechanics and society from the perspective of Scotsman James Bryce   Politics Pages 572

Stories of the Pilgrims *by Margaret P. Pumphrey*   ISBN: 1-59462-116-0   **$17.95**
This book explores pilgrims religious oppression in England as well as their escape to Holland and eventual crossing to America on the Mayflower, and their early days in New England...   History Pages 268

QTY

The Fasting Cure by *Sinclair Upton*   ISBN: *1-59462-222-1*   **$13.95**
In the Cosmopolitan Magazine for May, 1910, and in the Contemporary Review (London) for April, 1910, I published an article dealing with my experiences in fasting. I have written a great many magazine articles, but never one which attracted so much attention... New Age/Self Help/Health Pages 164

Hebrew Astrology by *Sepharial*   ISBN: *1-59462-308-2*   **$13.45**
In these days of advanced thinking it is a matter of common observation that we have left many of the old landmarks behind and that we are now pressing forward to greater heights and to a wider horizon than that which represented the mind-content of our progenitors... Astrology Pages 144

Thought Vibration or The Law of Attraction in the Thought World   ISBN: *1-59462-127-6*   **$12.95**

by *William Walker Atkinson*   Psychology/Religion Pages 144

Optimism by *Helen Keller*   ISBN: *1-59462-108-X*   **$15.95**
Helen Keller was blind, deaf, and mute since 19 months old, yet famously learned how to overcome these handicaps, communicate with the world, and spread her lectures promoting optimism. An inspiring read for everyone... Biographies/Inspirational Pages 84

Sara Crewe by *Frances Burnett*   ISBN: *1-59462-360-0*   **$9.45**
In the first place, Miss Minchin lived in London. Her home was a large, dull, tall one, in a large, dull square, where all the houses were alike, and all the sparrows were alike, and where all the door-knockers made the same heavy sound... Childrens/Classic Pages 88

The Autobiography of Benjamin Franklin by *Benjamin Franklin*   ISBN: *1-59462-135-7*   **$24.95**
The Autobiography of Benjamin Franklin has probably been more extensively read than any other American historical work, and no other book of its kind has had such ups and downs of fortune. Franklin lived for many years in England, where he was agent... Biographies/History Pages 332

Name	
Email	
Telephone	
Address	
City, State ZIP	

☐ **Credit Card**   ☐ **Check / Money Order**

Credit Card Number	
Expiration Date	
Signature	

Please Mail to: Book Jungle
PO Box 2226
Champaign, IL 61825
or Fax to: 630-214-0564

ORDERING INFORMATION

web*: www.bookjungle.com*
email*: sales@bookjungle.com*
fax*: 630-214-0564*
mail*: Book Jungle PO Box 2226 Champaign, IL 61825*
or PayPal *to sales@bookjungle.com*

Please contact us for bulk discounts

DIRECT-ORDER TERMS

20% Discount if You Order
Two or More Books
Free Domestic Shipping!
Accepted: Master Card, Visa,
Discover, American Express